Signs of Life

Signs of Life

Patricia Thoms

Cloonfad Press
Cassville, NJ

Published by
Cloonfad Press
PO Box 106
Cassville, NJ, 08527
www.cloonfadpress.com

ISBN 0-9744744-7-9

Printed in the United States of America.

To my daughter, Laur
Trust your dreams

Acknowledgements.

*M*y thanks go to my husband Paul for supporting me not only in the writing of this book but in my profession as well. Thanks also to my daughter Lauren and her gracious understanding of all the time taken away from her to accomplish this task.

Thanks to Rev. Karen Herrick, MSW, LCSW, who opened doors of spirituality for me and for encouraging me through the completion of this book.

Thanks to Raymond Moody, MD, PhD. His lifetime commitment to exploring the human history and validation of the human experience has been an inspiration to me.

Thanks to Jack Sharkey for agreeing to edit and publish this book. Without Jack, there would be no *Signs of Life*.

Thanks to Kathy Campbell, RN, Nursing Supervisor, for keeping a secret for over one year and allowing me to vent all of my fears. She remains a strong supporter of this book and her confidence gave me the energy I needed to complete it.

Special thanks to my patients, their caregivers, and my colleagues who allowed me into their lives and who ultimately gave us their greatest gift—caring and love.

To the spirits of Bobbie, Pan, Bob, and Barbara: I know your spirits remained with me throughout the writing of this book and your guidance made it a reality. You remain in my heart every day. I am grateful and I love you.

Foreword.

*D*ying people glimpsing heavenly realms of light just prior to passing away. Medical personnel seeing patients' spirits leave their bodies at the moment of death. Electric lights or household appliances switching on and off all by themselves in homes where someone has recently died. Birds appearing in some astonishing way that witnesses intuitively link with the recent death of a loved one. Signs from the departed.

They sound like incidents from a fantasy novel, yet these real-life occurrences are very familiar to certain helping professionals. Those of us who work with the terminally ill and their families witness incomprehensible, seemingly miraculous happenings on a regular basis. Still, we are understandably reluctant to discuss such events with a public that is ill-prepared to accept them and who may be harshly judgmental.

That is a sad situation. After all, the profound spiritual experiences of the dying bring great comfort to those who are afraid of death. They also ease the misery of those who are grieving over the loss of loved ones. So, I am truly happy that Patricia Thoms, a seasoned hospice nurse, has published this captivating account of her own spiritual adventures along the amazing frontier between life and death.

The phenomena she describes may well seem incredible to anyone who is reading about them for the first time, however, I can personally attest to many, virtually identical cases from my own practice. I am a medical doctor, psychiatrist and philosophy professor who has been actively studying the extraordinary experiences of the dying since 1963. During that time I have been privileged to interview thousands of individuals from all over the world who have returned to life after teetering on the brink of death. Planet-wide, people in that situation return to tell the same story of getting out of their physical bodies. They say they rise upward through a passageway or tunnel and emerge into a brilliant, comforting, light of love and peace. There, they encounter and converse with the spirits of their departed friends and family members. They see their entire lives reviewed instantly in a full-color, three-dimensional panoramic vision. They meet a loving being of light that helps them relive every single action of their lives and teaches them that the purpose of life is to learn and love. When they return to this world, they are never again afraid of death. They are not afraid because their experiences have convinced them that what we know as death is simply a transition into another dimension—a supernatural world beyond this one.

By now almost everyone has heard of these endlessly fascinating and inspiring near-death experiences. Medical doctors on every continent except Antarctica have studied and reported on cases of the phenomenon in their own societies and the near-death experience has been the subject of innumerable books, medical journal articles, television documentaries, talk show programs and popular Hollywood movies.

However, there is a lot more to the story that the public does not yet know. There are many other kinds of extraordinary experiences that take place on death's doorstep that are equally astonishing, equally inspiring and equally uplifting. These experiences, such as the ones Patricia addresses in this book, have not yet fully entered public awareness — and they surely ought to!

For example, it is not widely known that bystanders attending at the bedsides of the dying often have experiences of their own that are practically identical to near-death experiences. As the person in the bed passes away the bystanders themselves sometimes leave their own bodies! They rise upward toward a light with the spirits of their now-deceased relatives or friends. They say their goodbyes and return to their own bodies having accompanied the dying to the other side. Those who report these empathic death experiences feel that they actually co-lived the deaths of their loved ones. Not infrequently, medical personnel taking care of the dying experience this phenomenon as well.

Over the years, dozens upon dozens of doctors and nurses have told me they sometimes see patients leave their bodies at the moment of death. Occasionally they even see the spirits of their patients' deceased loved ones come to escort the dying to the world beyond. So, Patricia is certainly not alone in what she has experienced during her long career as a hospice nurse.

What has set her apart from many other professionals, however, is her courage in straightforwardly describing what she has witnessed and putting it in writing for the benefit of a larger, reading public. In so doing, of course, she has exposed herself to criticism from people who, not being able to comprehend such phenomena, are deep, down, afraid of them. Many people, including some medical doctors, feel strongly that these things ought to be swept under the rug.

Anyone who reads her book will realize that Patricia Thoms will not be deterred by any of the barbs that others may throw in her direction. It is clear from what she writes that she regards her profession as a sacred calling. It is my hope that many other physicians and nurses will join me in stepping up to the plate to support her in revealing what have become plain, clinical truths. It is becoming increasingly obvious that death opens a portal into a vastly important, unknown dimension of the mind — perhaps even into another reality beyond this world.

For instance, it is fairly common for people to suddenly start singing or reciting poetry — sometimes even creating original poetry — in the immediate days, hours, or moments before death. This happens even when these individuals had never before been interested in poetry as far as their surviving relatives knew. Not only that, the phenomenon was known to the ancients and is found throughout the world. Plato likened it to swans that, according to Greek belief sing the most beautiful songs of their lives when they realize they are dying. Plato hypothesized that the swans do so because they know they will soon be in the presence of God. So it is appropriate to refer to cases in which the dying sing or express themselves poetically as the *swan song phenomenon.*

Birds in general have long had a profound, symbolic association with death. It is quite common for someone who is grieving to instinctively interpret unusual behavior in birds as a manifestation of the lost loved one. It is as though they *know* that the bird's strange behavior has to do with the death. I have heard of hundreds of cases of this phenomenon and the experience Patricia reports in chapter nine is one of the best ever.

All events she writes about are part and parcel of being human and perhaps reflect our deepest nature. Many readers of this book are sure to be delighted to find out they are not alone, for they will recognize unusual phenomena they have also experienced.

Patricia Thoms has performed a valuable public service by bringing to light aspects of death and dying that are well known to many professionals. In doing so, she has also created memorable portraits of the many loveable characters she helped through life's final transition. I hope she is in the vanguard of many professionals who will be encouraged to report on their own life changing encounters with patients on the threshold of death.

I hope people who are fearful of death or of suffering grief, will read her book. They will find information and inspiration in it that is most helpful in coping with life's greatest and deepest mysteries. I thoroughly enjoyed this touching book. Take time to enjoy these most precious stories which Patricia shares with us all.

Raymond A. Moody, MD, PhD

Prologue.

It is with great honor and pleasure that I write this book. It has taken over twenty years dealing firsthand with death and the dying to arrive at this point. I have spent the past fifteen years as a hospice, or palliative care, nurse serving patients in their homes. Hospice care becomes necessary when treatment is either no longer successful or the patient and their family have decided not to seek further treatment.

As I look back on all the people who have crossed my path during the past twenty years, I am humbled and thankful to have met and learned from every one of them. I am in awe of the patients who so gracefully shared their most intimate fears and experiences with me. I am also in awe of the nurses who were dedicated to the comfort and healing of those patients in their most needy and vulnerable times and the physicians who were always willing to teach and learn about the mysteries of living and dying. These professionals all deal with the hard, complicated art of easing physical pain and difficult breathing, stopping the relentless nausea and vomiting, as well as making their patients comfortable when enlarging tumors are pressing on organs and nerve endings.

Professionals all, dedicated to offering strength when the heart is weakening, keeping the mind stimulated when dementia is overcoming the brain and body, and offering healing in the face of death.

I am in awe of the members of the clergy who were

always there for our patients and who were willing to be a listener, guide, or good friend. These ministers were willing to share their knowledge and continue to learn from all of us, especially our patients and their loved ones. Ministers whose business is the healing of a patient's spiritual needs have played a role equal to the medical professionals I have worked alongside.

Home health aides, always the hands on, loving practitioners of loving care are also a vital part of hospice care — giving their time so willingly to all who are in need.

Equally important are the psychologists and social workers who have shared their knowledge with us so willingly. They have comforted patients and their care-givers, including our staff, whose dedication to the healing of one's emotional needs is unrelenting.

There are many other people, family members and different practitioners of different therapy disciplines that all come together for the comfort of the patient and their families. The list of people I have a deep, abiding respect for is long and I feel it is important they all know how deeply I have been touched by their efforts.

So many people, so many lessons, so much to be gained from all whose paths I have crossed.

This book is not intended to review the hundreds of experiences I and others in my profession have experienced. It will not investigate the hundreds of spiritual events that have become everyday occurrences. Instead it will be dedicated to certain special events that have brought me so close to the other side that sharing it with others was too risky, lest it be diminished by their intellectual dissection.

I have recently felt compelled to share these wonderful, true events with others. My hope is that we can all learn from them and that those persons who have experienced like events can now feel their own experiences have been validated.

Because of the sensitive nature of my work and the desire to maintain the privacy of those whose stories are told in this book, times, names, ages, or diagnoses have been changed to ensure privacy. However, I assure you that each event as described did truly occur without any other alterations.

My desire is that this book will be a comfort to you and that you will learn to *ask* the dying for a confirmation of their spirit's survival after their body dies.

Chapter 1. Beginning.

I set my thoughts to writing this book during the summer of 2004. The past eighteen months had been an incredible journey of faith and discovery.

Approximately eighteen months before I started writing this book, I had met Rev. Karen Herrick, MSW, LCSW. She had been referred to me by my nursing supervisor. I entered her world in the hopes of simply receiving some parenting counseling. Three months later we completed that counseling but I had an intense feeling there was still more for me to explore. I asked if I could remain in therapy with her to work on problems that were not related to my marriage or motherhood. Little did I know the incredible journey I was about to embark on.

Karen is a therapist, an ordained minister, and director of a program for adult children of alcoholics. Much of this I did not know when I first started my counseling. What I would learn in the following months was that she was more than a therapist. She was my spirit guide and my friend in the truest sense of the word.

During this time, I was exhausted. For the past year I had been seeing my doctor with vague symptoms of fatigue. Many tests later, there was still no diagnosis. In addition to my constant fatigue, I had occasionally needed medication to calm my anxiety. I was now literally sick and tired of being sick and tired. I loved my work and the corporation I worked for, my marriage was solid and my daughter was exceptional, but there was something else in my life that was sapping my energy.

Fears of "nothing in particular" would not leave me. My energy level was alternately either surging or completely depleted.

Okay, I thought to myself, *I'll finally share how crazy I really am with someone*. I'll tell her everything so she can confirm that what I experience is not normal. I figured she'd tell me I need tons of therapy so I could once again be a "normal" person. Never had I discussed in detail with anyone what I was about to tell her, including my own family. Occasionally my husband would catch a glimpse into my world but I still trusted no one. I could not sincerely confide in anyone.

My logic was that since I was paying Karen for her time, I could accept or reject what her conclusions would be. If she agreed with me that I was indeed crazy I could go on with my life. I would accept that this was my destiny and the way I would have to exist until I died. My coping mechanisms were fine tuned — I could fake it forever. *Why not*, I thought, *I had been doing it for the past twelve years!*

I was also prepared to reject her conclusion that I was perfectly sane.

Here was the problem — my sickness — that was causing me to constantly live with a hyper-sensitive emotional system. Over a decade before, I had started working in hospice, caring for the terminally ill. I was a registered nurse with a psychiatric background. I had been feeling an overwhelming pull drawing me into this field, although I was also terrified at the thought of it.

In the early 90s, cancer claimed my younger and only sister, Pam. Losing Pam devastated me and the only way I could come to terms with it and accept it was to finally realize that I could not, did not, and would never accept it!

I doubted I would be good enough for hospice work, but I was determined and I was sure I could cover up my weaknesses or deficiencies. As a way to soothe the pain of my loss, I was driven to try and help those who would soon be suffering similarly.

I had the extreme good fortune to meet Doug Smith, MSW, soon after I started working in hospice. Doug is the author of *Being a Wounded Healer* and is also affiliated with the American Academy of Bereavement. The single most important thing he taught me was that I did not have to wait to be a leader until my education was completed or until I saw myself as perfect. He teaches that when we share with the dying our authentic selves, our woundedness and vulnerability are gifts we give of ourselves. That piece of wisdom set me on a course I could never have predicted. It laid the ground work for my thoughts and beliefs for the rest of my life. I was being driven to care for the dying and I was accepting that calling.

The staff members I worked with were all loving, intelligent, and spiritual. They all had come to terms with death and were comfortable with the thought of their own death.

Okay, I could fake this! I thought as I began my new career. After all, I had been a registered nurse my entire professional life. This was just going to be another phase of my professional journey.

The one thing in life I was never comfortable with was the thought of my own death. There had never been a more terrifying thought in my life. I never shared this with any of my colleagues. As a nurse, working with the dying was not new to me—I had been called to attend the dying in their final moments many, many, times before.

Although my fear of my own death was still with me,

I was comfortable attending to others in their dying moments. In spite of my own personal fears and discomfort, I was now being driven to take my service to others to a higher level.

I started working in hospice on the night shift. My primary responsibilities were to be available to respond to calls from our hospice patients and families and make visits when needed. Since my daughter was a toddler, this was a perfect fit.

For the five years I worked this shift, she barely knew I worked at all. I never had to leave the house until she was asleep and was almost always home when she woke up. It was hard on me but perfect for her, and I was grateful for this.

Within months of starting my work in hospice, I started to experience really strange events. My body, my soul, and my emotions could all predict what my night would be like. I knew instinctively when it would be busy or calm. I knew when to sleep and when to be awake. I knew when to nap, get up, take a shower and get dressed. I even knew when to remain available and ready to go as well as when I would not need to get dressed in my uniform to go out!

It was crazy and nice at the same time. I had a sensor that worked almost perfectly. My internal clock and prediction mechanism was completely reliable and only failed me when I did not pay attention to it.

I spoke to no one about this. I did not believe in angels, I had no knowledge of spirit guides, and I barely believed in God. I had grown tired of fire and brimstone so I had closed my mind and heart off to all religion and was completely resistant to any type of spiritual learning.

Spiritual to me meant religious and I'd had enough of religion! New age philosophies were not appealing to me. I did not understand people who were into New Age beliefs and never had any interest in investigating what they were teaching. I considered them odd and therefore dismissed them.

Still, my almost perfectly fine tuned intuition for my work continued to develop. At the time I did not identify it as such, but now when I look back upon my life at that time, I can clearly see it for what it was. Back then, I thought it was odd and left it at that. I was able to know when a patient was going to die or need me because they were uncomfortable. I had developed a sense I could not explain or share with anyone. I also never considered the possibility that there were others in my profession who had the same intuition.

The energy in my body would shift. It was like turning on a faucet. The higher the pressure, the greater I would feel the vibrations. According to these vibrations I could predict what was needed of me. This may sound like an interesting ability to have but I can assure you it was not a gift I would have chosen. I can only explain it as being in a constant, involuntary state of heightened or lowered emotional energy — an energy swing I did not control.

Occasionally I would be at a meeting and we would be discussing a patient. Even if I had never met them I would know whether they would die that week or not. I wasn't scared of this knowledge, I just let it be.

As strange as it may sound to someone unfamiliar with my work, over the years I'd had hundreds of wonderful experiences with the dying and so did my colleagues. Those experiences are gifts we all receive as part of our work.

But when I started to pay close attention to my patients who were struggling with the fear of death things shifted to a higher gear. These were all patients who were terrified of their coming death and—worse still—what was awaiting them after death. For them the horror was often too much to bear. I shared their terror with them, but only in my heart. Because of the differences in our circumstances, I could have sympathy for them, but I could not feel the totality of their terror. I was entering the world of spiritual pain that is sometimes suffered by the terminally ill. I was experiencing it with them and through them.

When I finally made myself completely available to these patients by suspending my own fears and beliefs I started to experience entirely new gifts. Gifts I could neither explain nor share with others.

I eventually started to keep a journal of these experiences for the sole purpose of being able to always remember these wonderful patients and their gift to me and their loved ones. As you continue reading you will see that these experiences were not things that could be shared with others in my profession.

Or so I thought at the time…

As the years progressed, I became more and more convinced I was crazy. After all, normal people do not live in a constant state of calm versus agitation. Normal people do not intuitively know when they won't be needed to help someone on a particular evening. Normal people do not instinctively know when the coming night will be filled with the pain and suffering of the people I was helping.

Enter Karen Herrick.

Confident she would diagnose my behavior as something falling into the *crazy* category, I was amazed when she told me what I was experiencing was *normal* for many people and that I was not crazy. She led me on a path of reading and learning about spiritual experiences and encouraged me to document them for myself. Her demeanor was matter-of-fact as she told me that I was indeed not alone, and for the first time in many years I began to relax and accept the things I was experiencing.

She told me about conferences where I learned about people who either had experienced psychic happenings or had recorded them from interviews with others. Looking back on this, I cannot believe I had never been aware of this world.

For the next eighteen months I followed a path of educating myself and slowly, so slowly, my confidence increased. To me it was like setting out on foot and traveling a very long distance to finally meet relatives I didn't know existed. People just like me — ordinary people with similar experiences. I am still on that journey and the people I meet continually amaze me.

This list would be incomplete without mentioning Dr. Raymond Moody, author, professor, and physician. Dr. Moody has written extensively and lectured on the subject of near death experiences among other topics and has been a pioneer who has opened the door to greater understanding and acceptance of the world we live in. I am grateful for the time I have spent with him. He is truly an extraordinary man who has dedicated his life to research and education regarding spiritual matters.

Karen encouraged me to take my experiences out of my journal and write them down to share with others. A small fraction of my experiences have been set down in this book with the hope that you may find more understanding and peace in your own personal journey.

The following is an account of those experiences.

Signs of life that came in abundance simply by asking for them.

Chapter Two. Sky.

In many ways this is the hardest and dearest chapter to write. Aggie was the patient who became the official starting point of my journey.

At the time I worked with this patient my spirituality was close to zero. Other than the death of my sister and grandmother, I had been basically spared the misery of dealing with the death of a loved one. I had entered hospice work as a memorial to my sister, although at the time, I was not consciously aware of this.

I worked the nightshift. The nightshift is a good place for someone who feels their skills are not up to par to hide, and I had no doubt my skills as a hospice care provider were not at a level that approached competency. I considered myself to be a totally incompetent nurse and was comfortable working overnights. Most of my responsibilities revolved around calling my patients to "tuck them in" for the evening.

Approximately six months after I started working the night shift, I met Aggie.

Aggie had been especially difficult for the hospice staff. Her pain had changed her personality and she had gone from being a loving, kind and giving grandmother to someone with an ill-temper who was intolerant of almost everything and everybody. Aggie slept most of the day and was awake virtually all night.

She was matriarch of a large Italian family, and was always the one who cooked Sunday dinner, taught the younger members of the family her cooking secrets, and in general kept her large family together. The ties of her ancestry were strong, and Aggie felt it was her special responsibility to pass those strong ties along to her children and grandchildren.

Aggie lived within walking distance of the beach in the very same house she had moved into as a newlywed, a half-century before. Her once grand neighborhood was now changing. Many of the big, old homes like hers had been converted into multiple family homes and rooming houses, and the area was in desperate need of a face lift. It was not a dangerous neighborhood but it was beginning to fall apart because of absentee owners and residents who didn't have the bond of ownership.

Through the years Aggie had often thought about moving but this was her home. This had always been her home. Her church, her neighbors and her memories were all here. And yes, the wonderful ocean she visited every day of her life. To her there was no acceptable place to move.

When she was diagnosed with stomach cancer it took a toll on Aggie beyond the obvious physical pain she was enduring. Not only was she growing too weak to stand and cook, she was increasingly unable to eat the foods she so loved. All the time she was growing thinner and weaker, her belly was growing larger from the tumor that was slowly taking her life.

Many times the hospice nurses would be called to make a visit in the middle of the night to adjust her pain medication. During the day staff members would visit and attempt to calm her and get to the source of her insomnia and increased pain, but nothing ever really seemed to calm her or soothe her pain. Eventually, it was decided that Aggie would benefit from a CAD pump.

A CAD pump is an electronic delivery system for medication. The delivery of medication through the pump is controlled by a program that can be changed as the need for medication changes. Since the pump would deliver Aggie's pain medication directly into a vein, the level of medication she would receive could be controlled more precisely. In addition, because her cancer was in her stomach, bypassing her stomach would likely provide better relief.

Each new level of dosage would be effective for a day or two but then the dosage would have to be increased. It was at this time in her illness that the duty nurse asked if I would make a nightly call at the beginning of my shift to speak with Aggie and reassure her that I was available should she need a nursing visit. We thought if we could reassure Aggie in the beginning of the night, her anxiety would decrease and she might be able to get some sleep.

When I first became Aggie's case manager she was not talkative. To her, my job was simply to fix her pain by giving her whatever medication she needed so she could sleep through the night. This is fairly normal during the first stages of hospice.

"You're probably not sleeping at night because you're getting enough sleep during the day," I said to her on my second visit.

"Damn you, I want to sleep *all* the time. You would too if you were in this much pain," she replied angrily. She had no patience for my diagnosis of her nighttime sleep problems.

Even with the input of everyone on the hospice team, she continued to require two to three visits in the middle of each night. During the day I sought counsel from the hospice team to guide me in the management of Aggie's pain and anxiety, but we were never able to find the root source of her insomnia.

Dealing this closely with Aggie brought to mind my own fears. I was unable to face the prospect of my own death—how it would come, when it would come. The thoughts of my own uncertain fate coincided equally with my concerns for Aggie.

On my fourth visit with Aggie I decided to just sit and talk with her. In the middle of the night the world is a quiet place and as we sat and talked, it seemed to me that we were the only two people in the world. I focused intently on Aggie's words as the rest of the world slipped away from my consciousness.

She was wide awake and told me how she came to this country as a young child. She still lived in the same town her parents first settled in. Aggie's parents worked hard to make their new lives in America good for their children and grandchildren.

Aggie emulated their loving model. She saved her money and helped each of her four children buy a home. She and her husband were never wealthy, but they lived for their children and scrimped and saved to provide them everything they needed and wanted. By living on a tight budget and saving as much money as possible, Aggie was also able to help her grandchildren with their educations. Aggie lived for and loved her family, but her pain was taking her away from them faster than her cancer was.

She had a strong religious faith and adhered to the religious traditions she had been taught as a child. She spent every Sunday and every holiday in church and she admonished anyone who strayed from their faith. She believed in God, Heaven and Hell, and the immortality of the soul.

On this quiet night, as we sat and talked, she shared

with me her deep-seated anxiety because she didn't really know what the soul was. Even though she had strictly adhered to the rules of her church her entire life, she was afraid she was not going to be allowed into Heaven.

Discussions with her priest brought her no peace, and in some ways only heightened her anxieties. She was told not to seek relief from pain, but to offer her pain up for the suffering of Christ instead. She was told severe pain was in fact a blessing from God. Eventually her pain became intolerable and instead of increasing her faith, the pain drew her farther away from God. How could she have spent her entire life serving and worshipping a God that was aware of and approved her suffering? If this was her reward on earth what kind of terror was awaiting her after death!

This was the first time a patient had confided her spiritual distress to me. *Oh, how I could relate*, I thought as I listened to her.

According to the traditions of her church she did everything right her whole life. She went to church, barely questioned its tenets, prayed, honored the religious and sent her children to religious schools. So why was she now so distressed? After a lifetime of religious discipline, why was she here in her final days feeling distressed and scared? Hadn't she accumulated a bank of good prayers and deeds that could help her now that she was at the time of her death? These thoughts began to overwhelm me as I listened to Aggie tell me about her spiritual pain.

This sounds simple but when I really allowed myself to listen to her I realized that I too had the same very deep, very definite fear in my own life. Sure, belief in God was important. I also believed that memorizing and reciting prayers were important. But I was now keenly aware that all of the things we are taught to do as outward signs of our compliance with God do not necessarily create a safety net for us when we are facing death. The great unknown is still a terrifying mystery.

There is no comfort from the terror some people experience when they are at this point in their lives. There is only one's self and one's God. This was absolutely true for Aggie. No amount of visits from her clergy could erase her distress. In fact, these visits only added to her terror. She also did not want to share her deepest fears with them because she feared that maybe if she did they would lose *their* faith, and she could not be responsible for that.

In her hour of need, she was alone. Completely and utterly alone as she faced what she truly thought was an eternity of pain and suffering. An eternity that would make her current condition desirable by comparison.

Once she shared her terror with me, it was no longer a mystery why her pain would be tolerable during the day and out of control when she was alone in the darkness of the night. During the day Aggie constantly had company and they all gave her some relief from the thoughts she couldn't escape. Her family protected her. But, at night when the house was quiet, she was left with her fears and doubts, and her anger toward God. At night she was alone in a quiet world that is not always peaceful but is sometimes a window into hell.

Her mind would fill with fear and disappointment over her inability to communicate with God. Endlessly repeating her memorized prayers was not unlocking the door to God for her. She had no peace and was convinced there was only more terror awaiting her.

The wall clock ticked off the seconds—a sentry performing a countdown as Aggie and I sat talking. She wanted to know what the soul was. She urged me to discuss this with her in her hope she could reach some kind of peace.

"Aggie, I'm afraid I have no idea. I'm afraid I don't have the answer for you," I said as the cause of her insomnia revealed itself before me. "I don't think I'm the right person to talk to about this."

I grew up not knowing what the soul was, although the vague, formless cloud that would undoubtedly suffer great pain in hell was a vision Aggie and I shared. Between the two of us, our understanding and spiritual growth was minimal despite the fact we were both raised in an organized religion that had definite answers to our questions.

Telling her I didn't have the answer for her, for some reason, encouraged her to include me in her quest for the answer.

"Well, then we'll figure out what the soul is together!" she declared.

Great plan, too bad it won't work, I thought as I took her hand and smiled at her. I decided to at least remain open to what she was exploring, if not for any other reason than to give Aggie some comfort and companionship during her hours of terror. Her pain was now stabilized and increases in her pain medication were becoming smaller and less frequent.

Although I had briefly encountered this situation before, I had never been the case managing nurse for this type of patient. I'd never had repeated visits and in-depth discussions with patients who were feeling anywhere near this level of distress. It had been easy for me to discuss these problems with a patient's nurse, pastoral care and social worker. After all, that was their realm!

This time was different. I could seek counsel from others but their effectiveness with this patient was limited.

During the day she was asleep when these other professionals — people who really knew what they were doing — were available but I did not want to interrupt her precious rest by asking them to come speak with her. At night, when she was alone and scared, I didn't have the resources those professionals offered available to me.

What can be done to help a patient like this? She wouldn't accept the spiritual counsel of her ministers, her doctor authorized increases in pain medication as needed, and a psychiatrist spoke with Aggie and offered to prescribe anti-anxiety medication, but the core of her problem was not being soothed.

Several weeks passed after our first discussion about the soul. We spoke a few times after that, but hadn't had a discussion with as much depth as that first one.

"Help me!" she cried one day. "Make sure I don't go to Hell! Where is my God and why is He allowing me to suffer so much? All I want is one short visit with Him to tell me I'll be all right but there is nothing but silence from Him! Can't you help me?"

"I would give anything to be able to give you an honest answer, but I just don't know what that answer is," I said. I was heartbroken that I couldn't offer Aggie anything more than that.

We were silent for a few moments but the silence wasn't terribly uncomfortable. Aggie was in too much physical and spiritual pain to worry about such trivial things as an uncomfortable pause in a conversation.

"Remember how we spoke about searching for answers together? Maybe we could find you some peace if we figure it out together," I said as I struggled to find a way to comfort her. I didn't believe we could figure anything out but I was desperate for Aggie to find the peace she needed to die.

When I first started working on her case I thought her only problem was her physical pain — and it was that pain that was causing her such spiritual distress, so I worked diligently to get that under control. But I soon noticed that even when her pain was under control Aggie still did not sleep during the night. She was sun downing — an experience of intense anxiety experienced during the late afternoon and evening hours.

Sun downing is a way patients communicate their fears and pain when their disease has robbed them of other ways to communicate to their loved ones or care-givers. In Aggie's case, terror about her coming death and intense pain had robbed her of her ability to share with her family her intimate thoughts and fears. She was angry and was no longer the sweet, caring mother and grandmother her family so deeply cherished.

Slowly, she began to trust my nightly phone calls. This happened over the course of several weeks and many middle of the night visits. Now Aggie knew if she needed me I would be there, and little by little, she started to relax.

One day I asked her what she did while she lied awake all night. "Do you read or watch TV? What do you do to occupy your time?" I was still trying to solve her insomnia without fully connecting to the root cause of it.

She looked at me like I was crazy. "I don't do anything. I just think."

"What do you think about?" I asked. I assumed she would tell me about her sadness over the fact she would soon be leaving her family and friends, her town and the ocean she so dearly loved. I thought I knew her! I was prepared to tell her not to try to sleep, but to do something like reading, knitting, or watching television to occupy her mind. I thought it might relax her so she could then fall asleep. It was during this conversation I learned to always listen deeper and not to accept the obvious answers I got from people.

"I think about death. I'm not worried about actually dying, but I can't imagine death. Where am I going? Will I know where I am? Will there be other people or will I be all alone. Is there really a God or is this just a story? Am I going to Hell?" She looked at me forcefully and continued to speak. "I am afraid I am going to Hell. I deserve to go there."

"What makes you think that?" I asked her. "You've lived a good life, cared for your family and neighbors, loved and worshiped God. Why would you go to Hell?"

"Because I deserve it. Even small sins will get you there. My priest gave me the Sacrament of the Sick but how do I know that will work? One little sin can send you to Hell, and I've committed many."

"Aggie, you've lived many, many years. We all commit sins, how could we not? We're only people. Don't you think God knows that? Don't you think He wants you with Him?" I said as I reached out and held her hand, trying to comfort her.

"No," she said. "I feel like He is waiting to judge me and He will look for anything I didn't take care of here."

"Aggie, I want you to think about how much you love your family. Don't you think God loves you at least that much? How many times would you forgive your family? What would someone have to do to you for you to stop loving them? Think about that," I said. My words came out easily and I was surprised at how much I actually believed what I was saying. I had never consciously thought those words before, and as I spoke them I was hearing them for the first time as well. I was answering both of our fears.

I was trying to give her comfort but for the first time in my life I was beginning to really try and understand how God thinks about us.

Aggie's pain was under control and I was spending more time changing the cassettes on the CAD pump than chasing Aggie's pain, and for this I was thankful. I sought out guidance from the hospice social workers and ministry so I could answer Aggie's questions, and was told Aggie had to draw her own conclusions. My role was simply to be her sounding board.

I now cared very much for Aggie. It gave me comfort to see that she was becoming more active and pain free. She was now able to walk short distances and was even able to cook some simple recipes.

Over the course of the next two months I saw Aggie an average of three times a week.

During this time we had dozens of conversations, and *we* came to the conclusion that our births were on purpose and that God wanted us here to do His work. We now agreed that our work here on earth was to fulfill our individual role, love God and love one another. Aggie now had faith that we would not be held accountable for our lack of understanding of the universal truths, and that God loves us more than we could ever love our children.

"After all, we merely carried the child, God created the child," she said to me one day as we sat in her kitchen and had tea. The kitchen was the center of her home. She had remodeled it a few years earlier and it was a truly warm and inviting space. Bright and shiny appliances sat comfortably among the quiet earth-tones and gentle décor. After knocking out some walls and expanding the kitchen into the area occupied by some smaller rooms that were no longer used, it had become a magnificent showcase and the main gathering place for her large family. Sliding glass doors opened onto a beautiful deck. From the deck you could hear the gentle rumble of the ocean and enjoy an unobstructed view of the eastern sky.

Slowly, my relationship with Aggie grew. From late summer through the fall and into the winter coldness I became comfortable speaking with her and no longer felt I had to have answers for her. We allowed each other to "free think" the deep mystery of life. Comparing God to ourselves as mothers was helpful to us because we could not imagine any situation that would cause us to stop loving our children. Yes, we could really hate an action but would never stop loving the child.

We decided that is how God is. Loving. We decided God is not the Wizard of Oz, waiting behind a curtain to snatch us and make us pay with our souls because of the lives we had led. He is love and love only brings good things.

Our conversations brought Aggie to the conclusion that God is not a sadist or punisher or evil being. He loves us and wherever we go after leaving this life was good. Now we at least had a framework to build on.

We spent much time talking about the possibility of life after death and what it would be like. We frequently talked on the phone and shared our individual thoughts on this subject. We finally came to the conclusion that we would continue to live after death and that our life on the other side would be meaningful and just right for each of us. God knew what we needed and wanted and would provide for that after death.

At first, I had a lot of trepidation about these conversations because I did not want Aggie's fate resting on my support. *What if we were wrong? What if I had given her false hope?*

Over the next month Aggie enjoyed a great deal of relief. She was able to leave her home for drives to the ocean and visits to friends and family. She was even able to eat small amounts of her favorite foods, but eventually the cancer overwhelmed her body and she became weaker and weaker. Death was coming.

"I know I will be at my funeral, and I'm going to be able to continue to help my family," she told me one day as she looked at a framed photograph of her family.

I was intrigued. If she really believed this, how could she accomplish it if she wasn't intact? She would have to not really die in order to do these things. She would have to leave her body but retain her personality, her memories and her desires.

"How?" I asked, wanting her to think about it. I thought maybe this would help her understand where she would go after she died. I thought it might also help me understand the same thing.

One night about a week later Aggie called our office in the middle of the night. She had been sleeping! Severe pain had awakened her and she wanted a nursing visit.

Driving to her house I was contented by her progress. Little by little she was relaxing and allowing the moments of her life to occur with less torment. It was good! Arriving at Aggie's home I quickly adjusted the dose of her pain medication and waited until she felt relief.

"Pat," she said, "I think I've figured it out! I could have waited until the morning for a nurse to visit but when I found out you were working I wanted to talk with you."

What a difference! She now had the face of a sage,

and she had decided I was the one who was in need of more understanding! It was great and it reaffirmed what I have come to know about the people I have met in my life. We change and grow and share and are given the extraordinary gift of our lives intersecting with others, if even for a brief time.

"I had a dream that I had died but was alive! I felt good and not sick. I could visit people on earth and everything was good. I was able to do the things I loved and my life was warm again."

I encouraged her and supported her dream. *If only that could be true for all of us*, I thought to myself!

Aggie went on to tell me she was all right with death now. She could enjoy her family now and had peace.

"Aggie, if after you leave here it's the way you just said it will be, would you give me a sign?" I asked. "Make it a good one so that everyone who is with me will know it's a sign from you from the other side. Let us know that we don't die, but most important, let us know you are happy and safe." Right then I knew that even if she was unable to give us a sign I would always love her and never forget her. This total stranger and I had shared so much with one another. We had grown to know each other deeply, without the usual masks we all wear with one another.

I was scheduled to go with my family on a vacation to Florida for two weeks and I was concerned about leaving Aggie. I shared my plan with Aggie and told her I would miss her and think of her often.

"I'll wait to die until you get back," she said calmly.

No! I did not want this! I did not want her to suffer one more minute of pain than was absolutely necessary.

"You go when you are ready. I don't want you suffering while I'm gone," I told her.

"We have a deal though." Aggie reminded me we had agreed she would give me sign if after leaving this earth, she continued to live.

I left on vacation sure in the knowledge that when I returned I would find out Aggie had died. What I did not know but would later find out, was that while I was gone Aggie told anyone who would listen about her promise to deliver a sign after death. Family members told me later that they didn't argue with Aggie but that they were all sure there would be no sign.

"After all, who ever heard of such a thing?" her daughter later said to me.

I didn't tell her I hadn't heard of it either but that I hoped it would happen.

I enjoyed my two week vacation and returned looking forward to my work. The first night back at work I went over the night's report with my supervisor. Five minutes after we finished the phone conference, she called me back.

"Aggie's daughter just called. Aggie's dying and she wants you there as soon as possible."

I couldn't believe it! She had waited! I prayed while I drove to her house that waiting hadn't caused her any unnecessary suffering.

Entering Aggie's home, I found a large group of her children and relatives gathered in the living room. They knew her death was imminent, and for the past two days hospice team members had been visiting regularly.

Aggie was conscious and able to speak very short sentences. "I told you I would wait for you," she said as I entered her room.

We gave each other a hug and a kiss and I told her how grateful I was that she had come into my life. I thanked her for her friendship. I left the room and her children were with her when she died.

The process of pronouncing a death can take an hour or more. In a patient's home all you have to go by is pulse, and even in total silence it can sometimes be hard to detect a very faint pulse. After I finally pronounced her death, I called the local police department who came to complete the report of expected home death. The family was in no rush to call the funeral home, as other relatives had been called and were traveling to say their last good-byes to their mom, grandma, and great-grandma.

I had promised Aggie that if I was with her when she died I would wash her and dress her in her favorite nightgown and robe. During the next half hour I washed Aggie and dressed her in her outfit.

It was now about 4:30 AM on a cold winter night. The sky was murky and snow was expected. There were probably twenty family members of all ages gathered in Aggie's beautiful kitchen, quietly speaking with each other and gathering their thoughts.

Suddenly I heard my name called, loudly and urgently. I hurried downstairs to the kitchen, thinking someone was ill.

When I arrived, everyone was on the deck.

"Look! Look! Look at the sky!" someone shouted.

Waves breaking on the beach could be heard clearly in the still night air.

Through the thick cloud cover of the starless night, we watched as a small circle of clear sky appeared. In the circle, a dark blue, clear sky with a single bright star appeared. Slowly the circle grew bigger and bigger until it filled half of the sky. The single bright star remained and inside the circle the sky was a dark royal blue. The sky was more gorgeous than any of us had ever seen. An airplane flew across the circle leaving its vapory contrail to drift lazily away. Then it seemed like someone gently pushed the contrail out of the circle with their hand.

Clearly, Aggie had sent her sign. No one had been out on the deck all evening long because of the cold, raw air. Aggie's son had decided to briefly step outside for a breath of fresh air and at that exact second the clouds over the ocean simply went away. Those in the family who had not been in on Aggie's secret were told about it by family members who had known about it. We were in awe and sure we were in the presence of the other side. The entire group was quiet and reverent. We were just "being."

Thank you Aggie. Because of you, I have had the courage to ask others to give a sign knowing that you would be there to help them along.

Chapter 3. Transition.

There is a wonderful town on the New Jersey shore about an hour south of New York City. People who are only slightly familiar with the town assume everyone who lives there is wealthy, but that isn't totally true. Like any community there are many residents who have owned their homes for many years and have worked hard to hold on to them as the value of their property increased. Over the years, as the wealth of the town grew and property values soared the perception came that now only the wealthy were fortunate enough to live there.

Enter Joe. He raised five children in a modest home in this posh community. Never poor and never rich, he and his wife Jeanne struggled to make ends meet. They were hard-working white collar workers who had always earned just enough money to get by. Over the years they had remained active in their community and were always involved in local politics, fund-raising, and school activities. Even after their children grew up and moved away, they stayed active in all aspects of their community.

Joe was a fixture in his lovely seaside town. He was committed to the town parks and helped plant flowers every spring. He supported the local theater group, helped organize the annual town Christmas tree lighting, and was always viewed as someone who was there for anyone who crossed his path. Although Joe was known by almost everyone in town as the person to call on in times of need, he was basically a reserved and unassuming person. After his death, his wife received quite a few letters from local shop owners and business people telling her how special her husband had been to them. Joe was a quiet man who was unaware of his importance and stature in his very well-to-do town.

He attended church all of his life and was very active in his church community even though he was not demonstrative of his faith.

Joe had been born and raised in the same town he and his wife had raised their own family. He joked that the home he had purchased for $12,000 so many years ago sat on property that was now worth $500,000 — without the house!

Although thoughts of selling his home and using his profit to buy a nice retirement home had been a frequent topic between he and his wife, there was really nowhere they wanted to go. As he told me early on in our relationship, "Nothing can replace our town, our neighbors, and our church." He had lived in the same place for over fifty years and he was happy.

In a world where everyone is looking for change, Joe felt he had it all right where he was. Looking back, I think he had been bestowed a tremendous gift.

All of their children were college-educated and successful and all of them lived out of state — far from their childhood home.

Joe was an ordinary man living an ordinary life in the midst of neighbors who were accomplished, famous, and wealthy. I first thought this would have left him feeling less than worthy, but it did not. He had grown up in his town and to him everyone who moved in after him was a newcomer, but he never viewed them as outsiders. Instead, he felt they were part of his community and helped them find the small town atmosphere they had come there searching for.

Joe's success may not have been measured by his monetary value but his work ethic, charitable spirit and quiet reserve made him a wealthy man in ways most people will never realize. Joe and Jeanne were a unique couple by today's standards.

Cancer was now ravaging his body and after a lifetime of quietly living his life, raising his family and contributing to his community, his life was slowly and painfully ending. All measures to save him had been exhausted. Chemotherapy and radiation were stopped because they were no longer effective and his pain was now severe and difficult to control. He was awake in pain every night but it was his anxiety that was truly crippling him. Fear of death was overwhelming him and no counsel by either his ministry or fellow congregation members calmed him. In many ways, Joe's journey was very similar to Aggie's. Joe also initially viewed my role as one of pain control and nothing else, and I had a difficult time trying to help Joe beyond that.

He had been in hospice care for four months. Pain management was successful for only a week or so and then the cancer would make his pain spiral out of control again. He required frequent visits from the hospice nurse as well as the home health aid, hospice pastoral minister, and social worker. All who cared for him were touched by this simple man and felt honored to be a part of his care.

As the days grew closer to his death, Joe was deteriorating. He was rapidly losing weight and his doctor prescribed appetite stimulants, but they did not help. Joe didn't want any food and was drinking only small amounts of liquid.

Day by day, Joe was dying.

Dying. Before my hospice work, it was always my understanding that we live until we die. We have all heard that death comes like a thief in the night, and we all pretty much believe this to be true. But many, many times this is not the case, especially for hospice patients. People who die of disease as opposed to trauma and who are allowed the dignity to die naturally, die differently. All of us who work in hospice experience this on a regular basis.

Those who are permitted to remain at home, free from needles and artificial life support have a very different type of death. Dying in peace, around the people and things you love is very different. Death comes in pieces, event after event.

The last time you can play golf… a little bit of death. The last time you can drive your car… a little bit of death. The last time you go for a walk outside… a little bit of death. The last time a friend from out of state visits you… a little bit of death. The last time you attend church or go to work… a little bit of death. The last time you can bathe alone... a little bit of death. The last time your child from across the country visits, says, "Goodbye, I'll be back," but you know you won't be alive long enough to see her again... a little bit of death.

"Goodbye, I love you"… a little bit of death.

Patients die bit by bit and many times they are the only ones who recognize the transition. Family members are so appropriately concerned with caring for their loved ones that sometimes the little goodbyes of life go unnoticed. Caregivers do not give in to death the same way the patient does. Hope for a miracle is ever present and a patient's loved ones live for that hope.

My involvement with Joe was minimal and consisted of just a few nighttime visits for pain management and a few calls from his family seeking support. I had very little to do with his care, but I knew him through our weekly meetings. I grew to know Joe's fears through the concerns of the hospice staff.

On this particular Wednesday night, I knew Joe was very close to death. Before I had even received my supervisor's report, I knew this night was going to be busy. The energy in my body told me so. I was now becoming comfortable with this odd new sense I had developed and I was tuned into it and accepted it. I trusted it because it never seemed to be wrong—it just seemed that I misread it on occasion.

I received a call from Joe's wife at 10:00 PM. His breathing was slowing and his family was afraid.

"I'll be there in fifteen minutes," I said as I hung up my cell phone.

When I got there, Joe was struggling. Restless yet alert, he was fearful of his impending death. On previous visits Joe and I had discussed life after death but it seemed he did not accept the possibility there was a loving God waiting for him. He was stuck on judgment and punishment.

I mentioned him giving his family a sign, but Joe dismissed me. He was convinced his death was going to be painful and horrific and that once he was gone from here there would be no ability to look back and give any kind of sign.

His fear was palpable. Priests and nuns visited him regularly and prayed and counseled with him. His fear reminded me of the religious tradition I had grown up in. For every bit of good news in our religious teaching, for every instance of happiness or contentment, there was some sort of punishment lurking in the background waiting to restore our misery.

I prayed for Joe frequently. I prayed that at the time of his death he would know peace and acceptance. As I took off my coat and got ready to help, I was disappointed because I just didn't think there would be peace for Joe on this night. Joe did not understand death and he did not want to die.

I gave him something for pain and anxiety and it calmed him down enough so he was able to manage some communication with Jeanne, but he was not able and not willing to discuss the fears that were overpowering him. Jeanne was all too aware of his fears and prayed for him all the time. Never did I visit that the rosary was not in view. I had been there about an hour when I left to make another visit but knew in my heart I would be back. Jeanne was praying deeply for her husband as I got ready to leave.

I felt very badly for Jeanne as I left her home. When it comes to death, religious ornamentation and tradition tends to fall by the wayside. No one understands how the spirit exists and lives and fear is the natural result of this total lack of understanding we all have about the death process.

I was a little more tired than usual so I stopped and bought a candy bar and a cup of coffee at an all-night convenience store. This wasn't part of my usual routine but I was just feeling like I needed a small boost to get me to the dawn.

The call came at 3:30 AM. Joe had lost consciousness. He was restless and his breathing was once again labored. I explained to Jeanne that these were normal symptoms of impending death but I couldn't comfort her, so I told her I would come to her as quickly as possible.

On my way, I couldn't help but think about what a beautiful night it was. I felt peaceful in spite of the tension as I recalled the story an elderly rabbi had told me a few months earlier while I was attending an orthodox Jewish patient.

I had been told I was not permitted to touch my patient after his death and that a rabbi would perform all the necessary tasks and remain with my patient until burial.

Since my patient had died at 4:30 AM, the burial would take place that day before sunset. I asked the rabbi if that ritual had started because people were afraid their loved ones may not really have been dead. This made sense to me because in the early history of humanity there were no EKG's to monitor the electrical activity of the heart, no stethoscopes to listen for the heartbeat, and no EEG to monitor the brain activity. There was really no valid, scientific method to recognize death except the apparent cessation of breathing and heartbeat. And even in the total silence required to actually pronounce a death, sometimes heartbeats and breaths are far apart and extremely faint.

The rabbi confirmed to me that this had indeed been the case.

I then told him how odd it seemed that so many patients died in the middle of the night. I estimated that probably half of our patients died before dawn. I had personally pronounced many hundreds of clients at their time of death in the hours just before the dawn of a new day.

"This is no coincidence," he said. "In ancient times the last watch of the day was from 4:30 to 5:30 AM. When a person died during that period it was considered a special blessing. It meant they did not passively die but were taken to the other side to enjoy the dawn of the new day."

I never forgot this and thought about it as I was driving to Joe's house. *Maybe he would have a blessed death.*

It was close to 4:00 AM when I got back to Joe's house. I entered Joe's home to find Jeanne, a friend, and a nun from his parish at his bedside. Joe was no longer responsive to verbal stimulation and only briefly responsive to touch. There were no respiration or pain issues evident and he appeared comfortable.

I sat with his loved ones for a while. We spoke of Joe's life and how important he had been to so many people. Everyone sincerely agreed that he would be dearly missed.

His wife was soothing him by caressing his arm during this conversation. All was well and she was clearly prepared for his death.

Joe's breathing started to change again. It became slower, with periods where he failed to breathe at all. I explained that this was normal. The breaths would become even farther apart and then death would occur.

Joe's death bed was surrounded by people who cared about him. He died at 4:30 AM, and I thought, *this was a good death!* It was a king's death for a man who lived simply but had died grandly.

Within seconds of his apparent death, before I checked his heart rate and pupils for the pronouncement procedure, we witnessed something that stunned us all and could only be called a miracle!

Just as easy as if it were an everyday occurrence, we all watched as Joe's spirit rose up—completely intact—from his body. In exactly the same form and appearance of his body yet transparent, his spirit rose up horizontally—the way Joe had been laying on his bed. When it was completely free from his body it became erect and then slowly moved toward the door and then out of the room. It took about six seconds from start to finish. Not a sound was heard. I don't think any of us even took a breath.

What had we witnessed? This was impossible. I decided that staying quiet was a good course of action. Death is sacred and I did not want to change Jeanne's experience of her husband's death by interjecting something I wasn't even sure I had even seen. I was also a little afraid I might have been sugared out from my earlier snack. Either way, I was certainly not about to share what I had just seen with anyone!

However, sometime during this we had grabbed each other's hands as we stood around his bed in awe of what we were witnessing.

Joe's wife was the first to speak. "I know I'm tired but let me tell you what I just saw." She went on to describe the exact same thing I had just seen.

We had all seen the same thing! What an amazing event. We all agreed it was a shame we couldn't share it with the world. No one would believe us. People would simply dismiss it as group hysteria.

For almost an hour we stayed together and shared our experience and we were all grateful we had been together to validate this miracle, this sign. As I look back on this scene now, I realize the only miracle had been our being chosen to see what our eyes generally are not permitted to see. I have since experienced several other instances such as this one. Instances I have experienced alone and ones I have been privileged to share with others as I did with Joe.

It seems possible that this happens all the time and that we are occasionally allowed to share it with the person who is crossing over. I believe a person may be able to control the way they cross over and are therefore able to leave us this gift if we are open to it.

After this experience I was told by some of my colleagues about a young hospice nurse who developed cancer. She was married with three children under the age of fifteen. Everyone knew on the night of her death that her time was drawing to a close but she insisted her children go to bed as if this was any other night. Attended by her distraught husband and three close friends who were also hospice nurses, she died at 4:00 AM.

Everyone who was there watched her spirit rise out of her body exactly as if she were getting out of bed to check on her children. She looked exactly as she had in life, except she was transparent. She left her bedroom and went to the door of each child's room, paused a moment as if she were saying goodbye and then disappeared. The four of them watched it happen together and later agreed on every detail of what they had seen.

We are dense and move at a much slower frequency than the spirit world. To let his wife Jeanne know he was going to be okay, Joe slowed his transition down just enough for her to witness it. He also gave her validation from the people she was with. This farewell gift from a loving and kind husband to his loving and devoted wife helped me on my own journey of understanding. Joe also left me a gift and I will be eternally grateful to him for that.

If I needed a sign to continue my quest for a belief system, I had just received one grander than I ever could have imagined.

Thank you, Joe. You may have lived an ordinary life but you died an extraordinary death. You calmed our disbelief and filled us with peace.

Chapter 4. Ageless.

Once in a lifetime one gets the opportunity to be of genuine service and bring blessings to a multitude of people — those close to the situation as well as those who are only on the periphery. Such is the case of the twin babies.

Being a nurse has not historically offered an avenue for spontaneous sharing of spiritual knowledge and it is only now becoming common. The general public might think that working in the hospice field would afford the nursing staff that luxury but it is not always so. Many of the medical professionals we work with, such as oncologists, neurologists, pharmacologists and surgeons, are clinically and scientifically grounded and are not always open to discussions about the spirit world or life on the other side. Such was our environment when our hospice team received a call from a local hospital regarding "the babies."

Generally babies and very young children do not become hospice patients. It's understandable that parents would want to continue any treatment for them even if there is only a slim chance of success. In addition, parents want immediate medical attention for any new symptoms that may arise. To leave an infant's symptoms uncontrolled is something parents simply don't do.

The hospices I have worked with have been wonderful with children and have all had an attitude of "no rules for kids." A child could be in hospice today and return to the hospital tomorrow. Parents lead the plan of care and the hospice team follows. That plan can change daily and that is acceptable.

Our staff had never cared for an infant before that memorable call came in to our office. A pediatrician from a local hospital was calling to report that twins had been born the day before — two little girls, Susan and Mary. One twin was healthy and the other was born with a heart condition that could not be cured with medicine or surgery. Mary, the sick twin, had less than twenty-four hours to live.

Their mother wanted her babies brought home. She wanted to be outside of the hospital and care for her babies her way. The doctor needed an immediate answer as to whether or not we could accommodate this family and provide nurses around the clock if needed. Although the staff was not used to dealing with this type of situation there was no hesitation. The doctor was upset knowing that nothing could be done for these first-time parents and their daughter and he was extremely concerned that all contingencies would be covered.

This was truly a first for all of us. No one on our staff had ever heard of, let alone dealt with, a situation like this but there was only one answer. "Yes, send the babies home." No one would be on auto-pilot for this case. The beautiful gift we all received was that we were all going to have to be in the moment for this one. We would all experience every decision, every action and every emotion for the first time.

A page was placed to all the hospice nurses, social workers and clergy looking for volunteers to be available in shifts to cover the next twenty-four hours. The staff volunteered immediately with no questions asked. The hospital was very reluctant and unsupportive of this plan, so a nurse and a social worker from our staff were sent to the hospital to get a report and help transfer the babies to their home.

Within two hours of the original call, the staff was paged again, this time with an unusual request. Could we pray and call others to pray for a miracle for this baby? But what would the miracle be? Should we pray for a reversal of the condition, pray for the baby's comfort in dying, pray for the parents...what could we pray for?

Prior to that time, I would never have called people and asked them to call others to start a prayer chain. In fact, my initial response was to scoff at the request but for some reason I immediately picked up the phone. I placed six calls and requested people to call others right away. This was an emergency and we needed a prayer network.

Once the babies were home, their parents needed much support. The twins' mother stated flatly that she did not want our staff in her home twenty-four hours a day, and since we were all certain Mary would succumb in the next twelve hours, we saw no reason to argue. We offered our teaching and intervention when she needed it, which she readily accepted but our general plan was to remain as out of the way as possible.

Both twins were being breast fed although Mary was too weak to suck strongly so any fluid she was getting into her mouth made her choke. This was a sign that her neurological system was too weak to recognize the need to swallow and that her throat muscles were weak. Calls were placed to the Pediatric Specialist who told us the parents had refused the insertion of a feeding tube for the baby. Aware that death was near they did not want to cause any unnecessary pain for their child. Our staff supported their decision and instructed them how to prevent aspiration pneumonia, which can be caused by inhaling foods or liquids.

The nurses reported that the parents were putting the babies together in a bassinet so that they could sleep next to each other, as they had done for the past nine months. Frequently, Susan, the healthy baby, would touch or hold Mary's hand. The staff said it was like she knew Mary was very ill and was saying goodbye. Mary was too weak to cry and Susan would comfort her. The staff reported that Susan seemed like an older baby and was remarkably aware of her sister's needs. Susan only slept when Mary slept.

These babies, these newborn twin sisters, communicated on a higher level than we adults and medical professionals could understand. As we all watched the babies interact with each other it became obvious it was innate, but where did this awareness come from?

Day one passed, then day two and day three. Mary's condition was stable. Their parents were happy about their decision to bring the babies home and were at peace with the inevitable.

Days six and seven passed. Phone calls and voice mails were frequent among the hospice staff—a miracle was in progress! With great excitement, we gave daily reports to everyone we had made our prayer requests to.

Days eight through thirteen passed with no emergencies. Mary was weak but no new symptoms had arisen. The miracle we had all prayed for was the gift of time— time for these sisters to spend together and time for these parents to watch their lovely daughters lay together and communicate with each other. No one could stop their tears of joy and sadness. Mary and Susan were truly caring for each other emotionally and spiritually. God was present.

For me, a dilemma had developed. I had no doubt

that a baby returns to heaven. For me there was no discussion about that but the parents were ambivalent about their beliefs. This often happens when death is close. Parents question everything they have ever learned. It is not a sign of a lack of faith but, to me, it is an indication of how truly human we all are.

I watched these children for thirteen days and was given proof that babies are not just little blobs of not-yet-formed people, but that they are truly the embodiment of homes for ageless spirits. The soul does not have an age, it simply exists.

Thoughts of asking for a sign entered my mind, but how could I even consider asking a less than two week old baby for a sign? That was a ridiculous notion I thought, but on the other hand I truly felt the parents would benefit from one. I decided I wouldn't be criticized if I asked. No one was going to come up to me on my judgment day and tell me I had gone too far and the consequence was that I could not be at peace for eternity. I prayed and asked Mary to give us a sign after she had left her body that she continued to live and would watch over her family.

On night fourteen, Mary's mother called. "Can you please send a nurse over right away? Mary isn't breathing well and her color is poor."

When I got there, it was apparent that Mary was very near death. I spoke to her parents about this and agreed to remain with them throughout the night. I told them I could stay with the baby or somewhere else in the home—out of their way, until they needed me. They agreed and several hours passed. Susan was sleeping for short periods and Mary slept fitfully most of the time. She was tolerating the oxygen mask but her condition was clearly deteriorating. Her parents and I were sitting in the living room with the twins and both sets of grand-parents.

Suddenly, Mary woke up and reached over to Susan. Mary held Susan's hand and they both smiled at each other. This lasted for almost one full minute. Susan put her hand on Mary's cheek as Mary died quietly, peace-fully and without distress.

Had we gotten our miracle? Indeed, we had. Mary lived for thirteen extra days. Thirteen days for her parents to say goodbye. Thirteen days for memories and pictures. Thirteen days for family members to get to know Mary.

Thirteen days to view the miracle and mystery of life.

We were allowed to witness the sign of two ageless souls aware of the near death of one of them and the communication and farewells between them.

Thank you Mary. Thank you Susan. Thank you God.

Chapter 5. Meadows.

One of the wonderful things I always enjoy about being a nurse is being able to meet my patients without any history or baggage. We don't ask and don't care about the background of our patients. Their personal history has nothing to do with our care for them. Are they good or bad? Faithful or a cheater? Religious or an atheist? Similar or different from us? Are our political beliefs in harmony or different? None of it matters. We meet as two blank slates, which gives us the ability to heal each other in a unique way.

Such is the case of David. I met him not as a hospice patient, but as a home care patient after I was brought into the case to manage his pain. David had been under several physicians' care for over six years but the unrelenting pain in his muscles went unabated.

David lived in an older ocean front community. Over the past decade many of the older homes had been bought so they could be torn down to be replaced by newer, more majestic mansions. David's home was humble. He loved his town and had lived there his entire adult life and to many people he was an icon.

While he had been a fixture in his community, and was well known as a business-owner in a busy Jersey Shore resort town, his life also had a bit of a dark side. He was a musician, was active in the entertainment industry in his area and was well-connected socially and politically. He was also a serious drinker and philanderer.

When I met David his legs were paralyzed and he was bed-bound except for the few times a day he was taken out of bed by a mechanical lift and placed in a wheelchair he could steer himself. We were able to bring his pain under control and I left the case only to be called back in six months later. Again his pain had surfaced and was much more severe. David could no longer get out of bed and could not hold his upper body erect. He needed help turning himself in bed. His bladder was weakening and he needed a catheter. His hand grasp was weakening and his ability to communicate was diminishing.

This time I needed more information regarding his diagnosis in order to put a long term pain control plan of care in place for him. After speaking with three of his physicians I had a clear picture of his condition. David had spinal stenosis, which is not terminal except in cases where the stenosis has reached the cervical spine. Cervical stenosis can eventually look like ALS (Lou Gehrig's Disease). At first it was thought that in addition to the stenosis David also had arthritis or another similar condition but David's disease was progressive and his muscles and organs were weakening—the stenosis had hit his cervical spine.

His family had been told about his grave condition, but because the disease had been so chronic they were not prepared to accept that it was now terminal.

Through the coming weeks David grew weaker. He had difficulty swallowing food and was soon unable to clasp his hands together. He coughed when he swallowed. The muscles in his face could no longer function and David was now unable to smile or make other gestures. These were all key signs that his body was preparing to die.

David had been a patient of the same doctor for well

over twenty years, and his doctor was at his wit's end trying to give answers and opinions to the nearly endless stream of phone calls from David's nurses and family members. David had worn his doctor out and his doctor was basically fed up trying to convince David and his family that David was terminally ill.

When I was brought back into the case, I decided to visit once a week and keep an eye on his pain and symptoms. His home care nurse was still available for his daily care. On one of my visits it was clear to me that he had inhaled food into his lungs. I called his doctor to inform him David had aspirated but his doctor was reluctant to accept my diagnosis. Eventually the doctor agreed David should go to the ER for evaluation, but he wanted me to inform David's family that if David had not aspirated he would not be admitted.

David was admitted for aspiration pneumonia and was hospitalized for two weeks. Now, not only was his doctor aggravated at the constant unreasonable requests from David's family and caregivers, he was also faced with the mild embarrassment that resulted from having a nurse provide him with the correct diagnosis of one of David's symptoms.

After he was discharged I spoke with David and his family about the pros and cons of a feeding tube. David and his family would only consider such a drastic measure "if and when the time came." I felt it had come three weeks ago, but his family was simply not prepared to accept that. David was not a candidate for hospice care because he and his family refused to accept the unavoidable fact that he was terminal. They still felt the disease process could be delayed.

David's wife was in her seventies and although not acutely ill, she suffered from arthritis and was unable to care for him by herself. Because of this they had private duty, twenty-four hour live in care for him. Sarah had been there for about two years and was now part of the family.

After some serious deliberation, arrangements were eventually made for David's feeding tube to be surgically placed the following week. During the wait his voice became so weak only Sarah could understand him.

David was terrified of dying and felt he had good reason to feel this way. Prior to this he had only been angry about his condition—thoughts of death had not yet crossed his mind. Now he was faced with the reality of his own life. He had not been a model spouse or parent. He had struggled with alcohol his entire adult life. He now knew he was going to Hell. He felt his family had many negative feelings toward him and would not be able to forgive him. David would cry uncontrollably, letting out an almost inaudible scream and say he felt as if he were starting to die. He would say over and over that he was too afraid to go. He had been in terrible pain and discomfort for the past four years but now he was filled with terror.

I tried to comfort him but was unsuccessful. David had a friend who was a minister who visited him every week for about an hour. I encouraged him to try to talk about his feelings with his friend, but David's need for comfort could not wait. I held his hand and said, "God loves you."

"I'm a sinner and I will not get into Heaven," he said with unspeakable fear in his eyes.

"God loves you," I repeated gently.

"No man is righteous and only the righteous will be allowed into the kingdom of God," he whispered.

"God loves you," I softly told him.

"I didn't keep the commandments and I'm going to

Hell." His voice was garbled and difficult to understand. It was also difficult to listen to—this pained and terrified voice of a man who was afraid of his imminent death.

"God loves you," I prayed out loud. There was nothing else I could have said to him at this point.

"I am going to burn in fire for eternity. Hell is purposeful physical pain and torture, and my eternity is fire and torture without end."

There was no helping him. The following day, during my visit David was silently screaming again and crying in terror about dying. He was not in pain and all of his symptoms were under control. He had decided against the feeding tube and his family was now acknowledging his terminal status. I completed the paperwork and admitted him to the hospice program. I remained with David for another hour attempting to offer him comfort.

Knowing his background and trying to divert his attention away from his terror, I asked him if he had ever gone to Radio City Music Hall in New York City. He mumbled that he had. I asked him to think about how the people stand in line, one by one, waiting to get in. The doors open and the people enter one by one—each arriving at a different moment to see the same show. I told him that life is like that. We are all in the same line and we leave this life one by one to enter the life waiting for us on the other side.

I could tell this didn't help much and I decided to drop the subject. I thanked David for the honor of helping to care for him. In his calmer moments I had sung him classic rock tunes from the 60s and 70s. He loved the songs and thanked me for the laughter and memories my singing brought him. I enjoyed David, he reminded me of my younger years. I was familiar with him and had seen him many, many times at various clubs and bars back in my younger club and bar days. He of course had never met me before and didn't know that I knew who he was.

Living at the Jersey Shore provides many great opportunities to go out and party and I was great at it! I have basically kept my friends from my teens and twenties my entire life. I have three older brothers and a younger sister and we would go out with each other and our cousins frequently. I always loved to have fun, and fun was always easy to find. David brought back those times in my life and we would laugh about them frequently.

Before leaving I told him I would pray for him and that if he was still frightened at the time of his death I would ask God if I could cross over with him. I told him I would pray about being able to help him on his journey. I told him about some of my patients who I had asked to give me a sign when they left this life. I told him I had received many remarkable signs from my patients who were trying to tell me that the life awaiting them was as wonderful as we dared to envision.

I was not worried about my offer to cross over with David. I wasn't afraid I wouldn't be able to come back. Those who have been able to leave their bodies and visit the spirit world know that God is not vengeful. He does not lie in wait to grab our lives. He is all loving and loves our trust in Him and would never keep us from returning to our bodies and lives before our time here is completed.

I left David after our brief conversation. It was late on a Wednesday evening. The following Saturday morning, Sarah called our office trying to reach me. When I called her back she told me she had taken the weekend off — her first in five weeks, and was now afraid David was dying. She told me he had slept all day Friday except for short periods when he was stimulated or crying in fear.

Sarah had decided to return to work early the next morning but right now she needed a conference call with David so we could both speak to him. The call was set up and David's family put the phone by his ear. I told Sarah that even if David was in a coma he would be able to hear and comprehend what we were saying to him. Sarah told David how much she had enjoyed living and caring for him over the past several years and I thanked him for coming into my life. Again, I told him I would pray for peace for him. I thanked David for all the laughter he had brought into my life and again told him how honored I was to have met him.

It was now 10:00 PM and I was enjoying a rare weekend with my family. My husband and I had planned to watch a movie at home and I prayed while I prepared a snack and cleaned the kitchen. My husband has been a hospice spouse for a long time and is used to hearing me pray for my patients. He is also well aware — as is anyone who knows me — that it takes me several hours to fall asleep. I never had the gift of napping.

We settled in to watch a movie we had both been looking forward to seeing for a long time. I sat on the couch with one foot on the floor and one foot on the ottoman and my body lying against the arm rest. This is a position I can't stay in for long, thanks to years of arthritis. My husband watched the movie and enjoyed his snack by himself after noticing I had fallen into a deep and uninterruptible sleep after about the first ten minutes of the movie.

In my sleep, I started praying for David. I was praying with faith because I knew where David was going. He was going back to his loving Father. In an instant I was no longer in the room or in my body. I had created a wonderful meadow in my mind. A meadow filled with flowers and trees and soft, gentle animals. It was sunny and warm and I thought *what a great place to be with David and help him!*

My thoughts turned to how I had told David that crossing over would be instantaneous and that he would no longer be sick once he had crossed over. He would be restored to a young man, strong and sure of himself with a strong voice. He would be able to walk and talk and feel wonderfully strong and healthy. In my meadow I told him — although I did not see him — that if his legs felt weak to call on this huge white bird that could help him walk by supporting his shoulder. This is all I remember except I knew I was not constrained by my body. I hadn't seen the bird but I knew it was there for him.

"We'll take it from here," a strong voice said, startling me awake. Through blurry eyes I saw that the clock on the VCR read 5:00 AM. A few seconds later, as I cleared away my slumber I realized it was just before dawn.

Again I heard, "We'll take it from here."

I was in the same position I had fallen asleep in. I felt relaxed and calm, with no aches or pains even though I had been in the same position for a long time. I sat for a few moments, enjoying this wonderful feeling. *Perhaps David had died*, I thought. I was a little upset that if he had indeed died he had forgotten to give me a sign. I laughed to myself and decided to go on with the day. There was a dense mist outside but I decided to work on my summer garden. The morning air was terrifically still and peaceful. Frequently thinking about the meadow while I worked, I enjoyed a blissful feeling. I felt warm and enveloped in the morning mist that was shrouding the coming day.

The next thing I knew the sun was warm but not uncomfortable. In fact, it was incredibly *comforting* as I knelt at my garden. Suddenly, a voice said, "Good work, we'll take it from here."

What had happened? I went in and checked the time and it was eight o'clock, but I didn't think I had been outside that long. Where did the time go? The phone rang and it was Sarah. She had arrived at David's home and was told by the family that he had been in a coma all night. He had awakened around five and told his family he was no longer afraid to die. He had visited where he was going and was happy. He asked his wife and children for their forgiveness and they told him they had long since forgiven him. He fell back asleep and died just before eight o'clock.

Where had I gone and what had happened? I don't know except I know I was not in my body all night and again in the morning. I cannot put into words this feeling except to say it was marvelous and warm. I knew I was completely cared for as I surrendered to the spirit world. Then I realized that David had indeed given me a sign but it was on a higher level than my earlier, earthly signs had been.

Thank you to all the spirits and guides who helped us accomplish this awesome transition. I will continue to pray that David ascends to higher levels of understanding and peace in his new home. I also pray that David will pray for and protect those of us who have dedicated our lives to the care of others and who are also waiting in line—waiting one by one to enter.

Chapter Six. Snow.

Sometimes a patient comes into the lives of the hospice team and brings us a great deal of joy. Such was the case of Sean. Sean Michael — his proper name, was eighty-two years old but looked like he was sixty. He was handsome and muscular and prided himself on years of exercise and good nutrition. His home was a beautifully appointed townhouse he was very proud of. Although he had out-lived all of his family and friends he remained active until his health deteriorated. He had no living relatives in the area. His spouse and siblings had died and as his disease progressed, visits from friends were becoming less frequent, but he never acted lonely. Most patients become very depressed when they realize they have out-lived everyone they love, but Sean's active life allowed him to keep his joy.

Sean had developed severe heart disease that was no longer curable. Although the disease was causing increasing, debilitating fatigue, he never lost his spark or sense of humor.

Eventually, Sean hired private duty aides who rotated on a live-in basis. The hospice staff would report at meetings that he was always concerned about his paid help. His top priority was making sure they were comfortable and well-fed.

Sean told me he had no fear of dying because he had a comfortable relationship with God. "I'm looking forward to the adventure," he told me in his thick Irish brogue.

He was very proud of his heritage and homeland, and frequently listened to traditional Irish music. In spite of his illness, he could still belt out a tune in a rich and smooth tenor. The staff all loved him. You couldn't help but love him.

Sean requested that the social worker from the hospice team accompany him to the funeral home to arrange his funeral where he selected the music and readings. He left a fair amount of money with the funeral director to organize an after funeral repose for his friends. All of his business was put in order. It was an Irish wake he wanted, and it would be an Irish wake he would have!

After that, Sean began to deteriorate rapidly. Again, I had not been a part of his care other than to call each evening and remind Sean or his caregiver that I was available should they need me, which I did at the request of the case managing nurse. Sean was a patient I had never met but grew to know through our weekly staff meetings and nightly reports.

St. Patrick's Day was approaching and the aide who was scheduled to care for him had requested a day off. The staff came up with a great idea: they found an Irish nurse who could also sing the Irish songs that Sean loved so dearly.

She said she would be willing to stay with Sean from 9:00 PM to 9:00 AM on March 17th. The only request the staff made was for me to make a visit to get the nurse familiar with Sean and let her know I would be available if she had any concerns. *No problem, this will be a treat*, I thought as I started out for Sean's house.

I arrived at quarter to nine and all went well. Sean was delighted with his surprise and after meeting the nurse I knew he was in good hands. I made tea for the three of us and sat with Sean while Jenny got settled in the guest room.

"I'm goin' to die soon. Probably this week," he said with the ever-present twinkle still in his eyes.

I asked him how he was coping with that.

"I'm a little afraid of dying. What if God doesn't forgive me for all the sins I've committed? What if I've been wrong all my life and there is no God and we go nowhere?" His questions spilled out rapidly.

We sat together and had an animated discussion about his perception of God. We discussed how we really are His children and how He would forgive us, just as we would forgive our own children. I tried my best to soothe Sean and it seemed to work.

Before I left him, I asked him to give me a sign if it was truly wonderful when he got where he was going.

He found my request entertaining and laughed. "I hope it's in my power to give you a sign." I assured him it would be by telling him about other patients who had given me signs.

"Pat, before you leave, could you and Jenny join me in Danny Boy one time?"

The three of us sang it with smiles and tears in our eyes. I left his home an hour later than I had planned. How quickly we can find love with total strangers. It never ceases to amaze me and will never become ordinary to me.

I felt strongly that Sean would die at the end of Jenny's shift. I reviewed the procedure with her before I left and told her to call me in the event he did pass away. I thought I might have been a little overcautious since they were both in an animated conversation about the west of Ireland as I left his home, but I had a strong intuition about Sean. The remainder of the night went smoothly and I called in my last report at seven the next morning.

I left a message for the staff telling them I would be available to do Sean's pronouncement even though it was now beyond my shift. The staff had their weekly meeting scheduled for that morning and being able to attend it would be a gift to Sean's nurse. At 8:00 AM I pulled onto my street—exhausted but sure my day wasn't over yet.

As I drove down my street it started to snow. It continued to snow as I pulled into my driveway, got out of my car and walked to my front door. My husband greeted me at the door and pointed out to me that the snow was only on the road and path I had just been on. There was no snow anywhere else!

"Someone dying?" he asked.

My neighbors, who were leaving for work, commented on how odd this was. I told them that it was fine—it was a gift from one of my patients.

"Must be Sean Michael," I replied with a smile.

Five minutes later the phone rang. Indeed he had died, Jenny told me. I returned to his home, in awe and delighted that he had honored me with his sign. Knowing Sean Michael's sense of humor, his sign was wonderfully appropriate. Years later I still smile thinking of my personal snow storm. He gave me a gift I have treasured for all of the years since I met him. He gave me a gift I will treasure for the rest of my life. Thank you Sean, enjoy your new life. May it be filled with the family and friends you missed so much.

Chapter Seven. Balloons.

There are times in life that you are thrown into a terrifying situation and come out staring God in the face. This was one of those times. This is the story of Doug.

Up until that time, this was the most difficult case I had ever been involved in. I did not want to case manage Doug and I practically begged the hospice staff to have another nurse assigned to the case. I was not a pediatric nurse and I was convinced I didn't have what it took to be one.

With Mary and Susan, there had been no time to be afraid. All of us were thrown in together to care for the newborn twins, but case management was an entirely different story. Mary was only supposed to live for twelve hours. Doug still had an unknown length of time of unspeakable pain ahead of him.

"I'm not one of those nurses who can handle hospice kids," I practically shouted at my supervisor through a veil of held back tears. "Take me off this case."

"Pat, you have to do this," she replied.

"It's going to destroy me!" I had no concept of how children died and I was not open to learning.

But it was my fate to be Doug's nurse—a fate I am still thankful for. I am still amazed at the power of things I don't understand that keep me moving forward on my journey of understanding.

Doug was a young man of sixteen. I had never been the primary case managing nurse for a teenager and I was still sure I wouldn't be effective. I was terrified! But I was on the case whether I liked it or not. Driving to meet Doug and his family I prayed that my nervousness would not show and upset Doug and his family.

This case really cracked me open and made me look at what I actually believed in. I was angry at God for letting this happen to Doug. I was still viewing God as Santa Claus and couldn't believe He would let this happen. Without knowing I felt this way, Doug taught me to love God no matter what. He taught me that God is only good and we should have no fear of Him.

People think nurses—especially nurses that work with the dying, are made of iron. We are perceived to be superhuman. I can assure you we are not. We suffer the loss and remember our patients long after their deaths. The difference is that we have chosen—or have been chosen—to do what we do and we love it. Many nurses will tell you they receive more joy than sorrow from their patients. I think it is a gift we receive similar to the gifts musicians and artists receive. It is a gift and we have chosen to embrace that gift and live the life it leads us to live. Coming to terms with that can be difficult though.

Doug lived in a nice area in a large split level home. His neighborhood was upper-middle class and well designed. It's the kind of neighborhood where the neighbors all know each other and kids ride their bikes on the tidy, tree-lined streets. It was late spring and the sun was getting warm. To see so much life going on just outside of Doug's home really intensified the apprehension I had about caring for him.

I was apprehensive because I felt inadequate. I didn't feel I could properly care for Doug. I knew I could get a lot of help on the technical matters concerning his care, but I would soon learn that the biggest thing I could do for Doug and his family was to simply *care*.

All my fear was put on hold when I first met Doug. He had no use for me! He would barely speak to me because he couldn't see a role for me in his life. Initially, this was fine with me. I could go about my tasks and wall myself off from him. I spent most of my time speaking with his mother. His dad was usually at work.

To him, my job was simply titrating his IV pain medications.

Doug had an IV attached to an implanted port site. A pump delivered Dilaudid though the IV. Dilaudid is a strong narcotic that can be safely increased as the pain increases. The pump is the size of a large wallet and can be carried by the patient.

Realizing that Doug wasn't interested in speaking with me, I joined Doug's mom, Sally, in the kitchen where we sat and got to know each other. She told me her son was a sophomore in high school and that he was a basketball player and enthusiastic member of his student body. He was just a kid — special in the way all kids are, but Doug was just a regular kid who was now terribly sick.

"A little over a year ago he complained about soreness in his right leg," she said. "His doctor said Doug had a sprain caused by over exertion from playing basketball. But despite several weeks of treatment, Doug continued to complain that the pain in his leg was not improving."

His family was locked into a health insurance program that would not pay for services unless they were ordered by the primary physician. Doug went for almost a year without seeing an orthopedic specialist.

When continued complaints did not convince the insurance company to give them a referral, Doug's mother brought him to a large university medical center to see an orthopedic specialist. Despite the fact that these services and any treatment resulting from this visit would not be covered, Sally persisted. She knew her son and she knew he wouldn't continue to complain without good reason.

Upon examination by a team of specialists, it was determined that Doug had bone cancer — the type that would have been curable if it had been detected at an early stage. That time had long since passed. Doug's right leg was amputated above his knee and he received a series of chemotherapy and radiation treatments to control the rapidly spreading cancer.

They told Doug and his family of his diagnosis and limited life expectancy and sent them home after his treatment. By now, the insurance company was more than willing to pay for any medical treatment, including hospice and whatever medications he was prescribed.

Doug was released from the out of state medical center and was admitted to our hospice program. Doug was going to receive at-home care, including a home health aide to assist with bathing, meals and to generally give Doug's mother a break from her constant attendance to Doug and his needs.

Members of the nursing staff were scheduled for three to five visits per week, or more as needed. The pastoral counselor would visit to give spiritual support to Doug and his family, as the social worker would provide the emotional support they would need. All these services would be under the supervision of our medical director who is a practicing oncologist.

I thought 'How could I possibly offer anything to Doug or

his parents?' after my first meeting with Doug and his family. Surely there was another hospice nurse experienced with this type of situation.

At our next weekly team meeting I begged once again to be taken off the case. Doug was showing no rapport with me despite three visits in the first week. I was strongly urged to remain Doug's hospice nurse and was offered all the advice and support I needed. I now believe I was destined to be in this situation and years later I am still grateful I remained on the case. Again, as had happened so many times before in my life, powers I didn't understand were leading me in a direction I did not want to go.

Eventually Doug became more comfortable with my visits. When he recognized that I was able to easily communicate with his doctor and adjust his pain medication to give him relief, he began to accept me. Sometimes I'd watch a movie with him and sometimes he would show me photos or home movies of his high school life. Doug was still enrolled in school but hadn't attended since the previous fall.

Ah, I can relax, he's accepting my presence. I wasn't completely comfortable yet, but I had stopped begging my supervisor to remove me from the case.

When you entered the new, large split-level home a small set of stairs led you up to the main floor where the living room, kitchen and bedrooms were. Another short flight of stairs led down to a large family room with a large glass-paneled sliding door that opened onto a patio. The room was comfortably furnished with light colored furniture and comforting dark paneling. Doug had taken over the family room to have more space and also to have a place for his friends to visit.

After a few weeks, the downstairs was completely converted to accommodate just Doug. He was able to see out of the large sliding glass doors which helped him to feel less lonely, and the morning sun coming through them was cheerful and comforting. The house was always immaculate and his mother admitted to me that she looked forward to doing the housekeeping—which she would do in small, short tasks while Doug was sleeping. She said it allowed her to focus on something other than Doug and help her to not fall apart as frequently.

I was seeing Doug five times a week for pain management and support for his parents. His pain was so severe that he frequently needed increases of his painkillers as well as additional medications to ease his anxiety.

Their home appeared normal but Doug's illness had taken a huge financial toll on his parents. His father was devastated by the illness but had to work hard to maintain his income and medical benefits. His mother had to leave her job to care for Doug full time. Doug's parents received some help from their extended family but were living on an extremely tight budget.

There were some bright spots, however. A nationally famous baseball player was in weekly contact with Doug. He would call on the phone, visit and give Doug secret signs when he played on television. Signs Doug could recognize as his own—a sign that he was being thought of, loved and prayed for. I was amazed at the generosity of such a star. No one knew, not the press, not his team or his fans, only Doug. He even came to visit Doug a few times and sent his limousine driver to a local ice cream parlor to pick up sundaes for the both of them to share while they watched a game on the television.

Another important life lesson: everyone needs to be a part of the dying process. Some to take, some to give. And all who are involved receive love and blessings that cannot be described.

The Make-a-Wish Foundation was responsible for this connection. What a magical group to give such gifts that even in the process of a terminal illness a young man can be so happy and a star athlete so giving and genuine!

One day Doug told me he knew he was going to die. He said he wasn't afraid but was terribly sad because he was going to miss his family, friends, and school. He said he felt like he was inflicting sadness and pain on everyone and sometimes he couldn't stand it. He told me he was angry his cancer was taking over his body. Doug didn't feel strong anymore. Day by day he was feeling physically weaker, but emotionally and spiritually he was stronger than most healthy people of any age.

Although Doug was a young man of sixteen, I saw him as a child. As a mother, Doug seemed to me to be too young to have to deal with his impending death. I had to do a lot of soul searching to understand that Doug was not a child but truly a distinguished young man, both in his school and his church. He had contributed to many volunteer programs and was leaving behind a legacy for others to follow. I was also beginning to further understand the age of the soul — among other things.

Doug was also a teenager, aware of his diagnosis and aware he would soon die. Many times after I would leave him I would drive and just cry for the injustice of it all. I struggled with my own anger over a God that would not pull Doug out of this.

We spent most of our time together working on his pain and other symptoms. After a while, Doug trusted me enough to start having conversations with me. I learned about his love for his school, athletics, and his volunteer work. He also told me about how painful it was to prepare to separate from his parents, siblings, classmates, teachers, priests and nuns.

We spent a lot of time talking about why we are born and what God is like. What does He want from us and what pleases Him. We talked about life after death and what it would be like. These conversations were frequent and I soon learned that Doug had come to firm conclusions regarding these matters.

During one visit Doug motioned for me to come to him. "Don't tell my mother I asked you this, but could you help me?"

"Sure," I said, fearful of what the request was going to be.

"My parents and I are planning my funeral and I want your opinion. I hate flowers, I can't stand the smell of them in the funeral home. They remind me of death. I want balloons, lots of them. I want people to know that God is good and we should celebrate. I want my funeral to be for kids. Would you help me?"

Sure, I would help him. *You don't need any help. You are so much stronger than I am!* I thought as I listened to this child plan his funeral.

Doug asked me to help him plan his funeral! I found this heartbreaking and awesome at the same time. He made me step back and learn the dying process from his point of view. He made me leave everything I had learned about dying and grieving behind. I became his student.

The songs, the liturgy, the pallbearers, and finally the decorations were selected.

During his illness balloons were his favorite presents. If he wanted balloons at his funeral, then balloons it would be! His parents agreed and were delighted. We reminded Doug that we couldn't release the balloons because they posed a danger to birds and other wildlife, and Doug didn't bother to remind us that he was fully aware of that fact.

Sometimes Doug would cry quietly with me and always say, "Don't tell my mom. She'll only worry."

He would always say his tears were because he didn't want to leave. He couldn't imagine being without his family, friends, teachers and things he loved.

"Do you think we eat in Heaven? Or play sports, or go to school?"

"Are these things you want to do in Heaven?" I asked.

"Absolutely! I want to keep on living."

"Then Doug, you need to pray and ask God what life will be like in Heaven."

Doug had absolute faith in God and no fear of punishment. He believed God dearly loved him and whatever was in store for him would be based in that love. His faith was unshakeable. Nuns and priests who were his teachers would leave his home crying saying they wished they had half the faith he had.

One day Doug asked, "What do you think happens to us after death?"

I told him I wasn't sure but I had a feeling he himself would be teaching us.

"I would give anything not to die. I want to stay here so much. I cry when no one is looking," he said as tears welled up in his eyes.

I told him it would be all right to cry with the people he loved. "Sometimes people are afraid to be around someone who is sick. They're afraid to cry or they're afraid they'll make you feel worse. But crying gives people the ability to share your journey with you. Think about it

Doug, and if it feels right, try it."

Then we both cried until it hurt.

"Thank you Doug for sharing with me. I am learning so much from you."

Doug started calling me his "angel," and as his illness progressed I agreed to be available to him twenty-four hours a day if he needed me. This happened a few times.

On one occasion, after his pain was under control, his parents went to bed and Doug and I sat up and talked.

"You believe in God, right?" Doug asked me. "What do *you* think He's like?"

He didn't realize what a loaded question this was for a person who hadn't quite figured that all out yet!

"Tell me Doug, what do you believe?" I said without answering.

"I believe that God is my Father and just like my parents He loves me so much. I really believe God is sad I'm sick but He will take care of me when I go home to Him."

"How will He take care of you?" I asked.

"I'm not sure, I just know I'll be happy and protected by Him."

"Do you think there will be other kids with you?"

"I hope so. I don't like to be alone," he said with the kind of smile only a teenager is capable of smiling.

Thinking of Aggie, I said, "Why don't you ask God tonight to give you a dream and let you know some of the answers to your questions?"

The sicker Doug got, the more frequently I was called to his home. It became a common occurrence for me to be sitting cross-legged on the floor with Doug lying on the couch.

"Pat, could you promise me something?" he asked one night.

"Sure, Doug. Anything."

"When I die would you make sure I'm clean and dress me in my school sweats?"

"Sure, Doug, I just hope I'm with you when you die."

"You will be," he said.

"How do you know?" I asked.

"Because I asked for it and I know you'll be here." The silence of the night interrupted our conversation for a few moments as I thought about what Doug had just said.

"What happens as soon as a person dies?" he asked, breaking the silence.

I explained that I would listen to his heart and lungs to make sure his breathing and heart had stopped. I would check his eyes to make sure there was no brain activity. I told him I would then gently wash and dress him. I told him we would call the funeral director when his parents were ready and I would help put him on a stretcher and into the van.

"Pat, promise me you'll stay no matter how long that takes."

"I promise you Doug." I knew I could keep this promise because my angel would make sure I wasn't needed anywhere else at that time. "I'll honor and care for your body, Doug, and I'll make sure things go correctly."

Doug wanted to know all the details about his last minutes at home and frequently interrupted me with questions. When I finished, Doug was satisfied he would be well taken care of and his parents would not be left alone.

"See, I'm hurting you too with this dying business and I'm sorry about that," he said.

"I choose to do the work I do and even though it gets really sad sometimes, I'm always glad I do it."

"I will remember you, Pat," he said.

And I knew he would. I asked him about giving me a

sign and told him about the other signs I had received. He really liked this. A project he could do after leaving the earth! It intrigued him. He promised to give me a sign if he was able and I promised not to make a judgment if there was no sign. Maybe he wouldn't be able to give a sign and I wouldn't interpret that as a sign that he wasn't okay. I didn't want him to worry about giving me the sign.

We laughed about the kind of sign because I was very clear that it must be obvious and beyond the natural so that everyone who witnessed it would know Doug was there and telling us his new life was good and he was happy.

I shared this with his parents and although they did not interfere, I felt they were placating us. I often wondered what they thought about me — this stranger who was taking care of their terminally ill son and who was now expecting a sign from him after he had died!

Doug was now having friends over less frequently because he was so sick. He wanted to spend his awake time with his family. He told me he had been thinking of telling his friends he would do this and I encouraged him to tell them that so they wouldn't misinterpret his withdrawal.

Kids tend to blame themselves too easily and his friends might have felt they had annoyed Doug.

The day before he died I was called to his home. His pain was out of control and Doug was asking for me. Despite elevating the narcotic dosage we weren't satisfied with his relief. I called his doctor who arrived at Doug's home at 1:00 AM. He changed the dosage allowance for the pain medication and within thirty minutes Doug was comfortable, but still anxious.

I did meditation with him and he eventually closed his eyes and rested. That night I could not leave him. Although hospice nurses normally do not remain with a patient in their home, on this night I thought it was the right thing to do. The rest of the night I sat on the floor, staring at him, praying for him and wrestling with the God he so loved. His mom never left him, and his dad stayed with him until he had to get ready to leave for work before dawn the next morning.

I prayed for Doug's dad because of all he was being forced to miss. I knew it was difficult to work in a demanding job every day knowing your young son was about to leave your life for good. For over twelve hours a day, Dad was not allowed to grieve, not allowed to cry, not allowed to scream out loud. His family needed his income and benefits. My heart really hurt for this family.

Just before dawn Doug woke up and asked for his parents. He told them he knew he was going to die now and wanted to say goodbye, and as easily as that he died.

After Doug died I carried out all his wishes. I carefully washed his body and helped dress him. I pronounced his death and signed his death certificate. When the funeral director got to the house, I stayed with Doug while he was placed in the hearse. His parents were too upset to accompany him. I was too, but I had made a promise, so I stayed with him until the door of the hearse was closed.

As the hearse pulled away I couldn't cry. How can a person cry when all they want to do is scream? At that moment, I had a true one-on-one fight with God.

"You'd better be all You say You are. You'd better take care of this child."

The gentle outside noise of the living was all that answered me. The hum of cars, birds calling from the trees, a child shouting.

"If You don't, You will have to deal with me!"

The only response was the soft breeze and the gentle

hum of the living world. My anger and grief was frightening to me because I had always treated God as a non-person who may or may not have been real. Now I was challenging Him — daring Him — to take care of this child.

I began to listen to the beauty of the living world and I realized it was God's response to me. Death was a part of life and I had an important gift — a gift of comfort for people who were being forced to confront the unthinkable.

This was the exact moment my life changed. This was the moment I made the conscious decision to stay with hospice and devote my life to it.

Doug had been better off with me in his life.

We are all faced with tasks that at first seem insurmountable and unnecessary.

The day of Doug's funeral arrived and after saying goodbye in the funeral home, hundreds of people began to form the incredibly long line of cars that would escort Doug to his funeral.

Nurses, classmates, teachers, friends, and florists had all conspired to fill this day with balloons. The police escorts had balloons tied together in bouquets on their motorcycles. So did the hearse, limousines and all the cars! It was a sight to behold. The colors of Doug's school were being driven through the streets of Doug's town to Doug's church.

Slowly the caravan moved. Hearts broken. Hearts too heavy to think. Even I, a relative stranger, was overwhelmed with sadness.

We arrived at the church and the banisters along the steps were covered with bouquets of balloons. Doug's classmates had prepared a program for the service and they gently and sadly handed one to each of the attendees as they entered. Inside, the altar was filled with bouquets of balloons and looked beautiful in its sadness. The centerpiece by the casket was a large Mylar balloon in the shape of a gondola with a large hot-air balloon on top.

Over seven hundred people were there.

Upon completion of the funeral mass, Doug's casket was escorted down the church aisle by his female classmates. I trembled at their sadness, maturity, and braveness. Surely, at this moment, they were as brave as any soldier. We ask so much of the young and amazingly they come through for us often less able adults.

Without warning, his classmates began to sing Doug's favorite song. It wasn't listed in the program and it wasn't a "church" song, but the beauty and simplicity was overwhelming. His friends had taken over the closing of the service and they had honored their classmate magnificently.

As the casket passed through the open doors of the church a wind we must have been too preoccupied to notice pulled the balloons free from the banisters. The balloons all sailed into the air.

The caravan then headed for the cemetery. As we drove, the balloon bouquet tied to the motorcycle leading us broke away and flew into the air. Now, one by one, the balloons on the cars all began to break away. *What was happening?*

We arrived at the graveside and a huge amount of balloons were delivered to surround Doug. It was as if every single person that had ever met Doug or his family had gone and ordered *twice* as many balloons as they thought were enough to express their sadness. During the service balloons began breaking away, one by one, flying up in the air on the stiff breeze. No one escaped what was happening.

Finally the service was over and as everyone said their one last goodbye, the large Mylar hot-air balloon broke free and slowly moved over to Doug's family. It hovered low and then flew just a little higher. People were gasping. Then after what seemed an eternity, the balloon gently flew higher and then suddenly, as if with a burst of energy, flew so high it could no longer be seen.

People were talking out loud about the balloons. I couldn't help but imagine Doug, with that precious smile of his, guiding the balloon and enjoying himself immensely.

The police officers who had escorted the funeral procession said their bouquets had broken off as if they were cut — ribbon still remained tied to their motorcycles. We then took notice that the ribbons were still tied to the antennas on our cars and they too seemed to have been cut.

Thank you Doug. Thank you for coming into our lives, and thank you for your sign. Those of us you left behind needed to know that God is good and present and is always with you and with us.

Goodbye Doug. Never, ever, will I forget the lessons you taught me and the faith you instilled in me. To this day I cry when I think about you. Not because I am afraid for you but because, for me, you were an angel on earth. You allowed me into your life and shared your most intimate thoughts. We trusted each other. Goodbye Doug. I love you. Take care of the other kids that go to the other side without the benefit of your faith and understanding.

We will meet again.

Chapter Eight. Silent Night.

For Christians all over the world, Christmas Eve is a special, holy time. Despite all of the cultural forces at work on us at this time of year with the presents, decorations and parties, in the quiet of the day it remains magic.

As a nurse, there are no guarantees of holiday rest. When we choose the profession we know that but it doesn't make it any easier when it's your turn to work on Christmas Eve. I started this particular Christmas Eve recognizing that I was the fortunate one. This year it was not my loved one who was facing death as it had been in the recent past. I offered the evening up to that recognition.

I was now becoming comfortable with my abilities to help and comfort my patients and their families. I was tuned in to my intuition, and more often than not allowed it to guide me through me shifts.

Shortly after starting my shift and receiving the report from my supervisor I received a call from the daughter of a patient who had recently been admitted into hospice. The patient, who's name was Antoinette had breast cancer that had spread throughout her body. Antoinette's daughter told me her mother was starting to have difficulty breathing. Unable to reassure her over the phone, I decided to make a home visit.

I relaxed and listened to Christmas music on the radio during the forty minute drive. The roads were quiet and there was that special, magical peace in the air that is reserved for special nights. My intuition told me to prepare for a long evening.

Entering the driveway, I immediately felt the sadness of this moment for this family I had never met before. Our client was staying with her daughter in her daughter's lovely new home which was decorated beautifully for the holiday. Later, her daughter told me this was a special request from Antoinette — she wanted her children to have a joyous Christmas with good memories, despite her illness.

I was met at the door by Karen, the daughter Antoinette was living with. Karen ushered me in and introduced me to her two brothers and one sister, their spouses and their children. She then took me upstairs.

Antoinette was lying in her bed on top of her covers. She was dressed in a Christmas sweatshirt with red slacks. The lights in the room were soft and the air was still. Had she not been ill, she would have been the grand hostess of the party downstairs.

Her breathing was labored and although she was weak, she was alert and talking. I instructed Antoinette and her family how to use her medications to ease her discomfort. I gave them information on the appropriate dose to ease Antionette's shortness of breath but still keep her alert. Satisfied with the results, I went downstairs.

The family was appropriately sad and very concerned. I explained to them the expected symptoms and how to manage their mother's impending death.

Antoinette's youngest son, John, was visibly upset and became quite agitated at me. He was angry he was losing his mother and the fact that it was Christmas Eve only served to heighten and magnify his pain. It's not uncommon for a family member — particularly a child of the patient — to take their anger and pain out on those of us who come to help, and I didn't allow myself to get hurt or offended by his words. It is accepted by all of us in this profession as part of the job.

"Why are you even here if you can't do anything else but tell us Mom is going to die?" John said sharply.

"There is nothing anyone can do. This is just part of the process your mom is going through," I said as softly as possible. The tension in the living room was thick. The rest of Antoinette's family was prepared for the inevitable but they were just too sad to do anything but stand by and listen as John vented his anger.

"There is nothing anyone can do," he snapped sarcastically. "You're all a bunch incompetents who couldn't fix a headache. You're wasting time while our mother is upstairs unable to breathe. Why don't you just get out of here and call someone who knows what they're doing?"

"John, please calm down," Karen finally said.

With that, John turned and walked past the beautiful Christmas tree into the kitchen.

"I'm sorry," Karen said to me. "Please, finish what you were saying."

"Karen, please, there is no reason to apologize. This is a difficult time for everyone," I said and then continued to explain the medications and how they worked. I also advised them that if they could not emotionally handle Antoinette's transition, I could make arrangements to move her to our inpatient facility. That immediately calmed the family. Their mother would remain with them—she would die at home.

I left the family a brochure explaining what changes were occurring to the body to cause each symptom and what to expect at the time of death. I left the house just before 11:00 PM, content I had taught them everything I could. I said a prayer asking for Antoinette's death to be peaceful.

I had driven almost twenty miles before my pager went off. The service advised me that Antoinette's family was calling. I called her daughter and she told me what was happening. I told her that her mother's death was imminent, and Karen asked me to come back to the house. I turned the car around and headed immediately back to Antoinette and her family.

When I got there the family was crying and it was obvious John was still quite angry.

"The Death Angel is back. Why are *you* here again, you idiot?" John said as I entered the home. "It's too late for you people to do anything now, so why are you here?" John demanded again as I took off my coat. "What are you going to do now, speed her death up with more of your useless medication?"

I understood his pain but there was nothing I could say to comfort him. John lived in another state and had not been able to care for his dying mother. He was not prepared for her death and that was the root of his pain.

I went upstairs to Antoinette. She did not respond to any of my stimulations and appeared to be comatose. I explained to her family that even though she could not speak, she could hear and understand everything that was said to her and she would be able to tell who was speaking. I explained that it was not too late to speak with her. I quietly prayed for her and asked her to give this wonderful, loving family a sign when she crossed over.

I shared this prayer and request with Joan, Karen's sister, who was open and comfortable with her mother's imminent death. As the family came up to say goodbye, some of them politely requested I go downstairs so they could be alone with Antoinette.

I went downstairs, where Karen had a cup of tea waiting for me. I passed the Christmas tree and the warm fire in the fireplace. The mantle was covered with picture after picture of Antoinette's warm and loving family.

In the kitchen the sadness hit me like a wall of heat. Death is hard enough but on a night like tonight it seemed too much to ask this family to bear.

John came into the kitchen a few moments later. He was calmer now — his sadness had overwhelmed his anger.

"Please, isn't there anything you could do to keep her from dying tonight," he gently asked me as he leaned against the counter. It was obvious he had been crying and that he had stopped masking his broken heart with his anger. "She has worked too hard and been too faithful to God to die tonight."

"John, I know this is probably the most difficult thing to have to go through, especially on this night. But, even if it was in my power to reverse Antionette's death tonight, would you want me to? Would you want your mom to celebrate the birth of Jesus with Christmas lights and tinsel, and music from the stereo or would you rather she celebrate it in Heaven? Do the presents and traditions of your family take the place of being in the home of Jesus tonight? Are the carols on the stereo more joyous than the ones sung by angels?" I sat at the table and put milk in my tea and hoped my words could somehow soothe this aching soul.

"No," he finally said. "She should be with God tonight. She has been faithful all of her life and I guess He has called her home." John and I were alone in the kitchen. The children were all asleep and the other adults were all upstairs with Antoinette.

Suddenly we noticed darkness and quiet in the living room. John went to investigate and found that the lights on the Christmas tree had gone off. He checked the switch and shook the wires, but the lights would not come back on. The tree was dark and the stereo was off and would not come back on.

A few seconds later, Karen called for John and me to come upstairs. Antoinette was relaxed and breathing normally. With her eyes open, she said goodbye and wished everyone a loving Christmas.

She did not take another breath.

There was no struggle, no air hunger, and no anxiety. She simply did not take the next breath. I sat with her for quite a while before I pronounced her death.

The family called the funeral director who arrived within the hour. Feeling they had sufficiently said their goodbyes, they permitted Antoinette to leave the home with him.

As the stretcher crossed the threshold, with everyone in Antoinette's family there to bid her farewell, the lights on the Christmas tree suddenly came on. 'O Holy Night' started playing softly from the stereo. No one was anywhere near any of the switches or plugs.

To give a sign to her family, Antoinette took control of the electric circuits that powered the tree and the stereo. Her Christmas present to her family was the huge smile she gave them, along with a sign that she had not died but was going to be with them always.

I left that night thanking God I had worked and seen His power one more time. I smiled thinking of Antoinette and how it must be true that we do not die but remain intact on the other side. A sense of awe struck me at how kind God is to care about us in our grief and let us know that all is well. I quietly drove to my next patient, awash in the incredible emotion. I knew I could not share this event with anyone just yet. It belonged to Antoinette and her family. All I could do right now was just "be" and enjoy the sign and reassurance I had just received on this special night.

Thank you Antoinette for the gift you gave to all of us who were there on that most precious Christmas Eve.

Chapter 9. Cardinals.

In the early stages of the AIDS crisis, those of us in the medical profession had many complications to deal with. Besides the fact that no one knew the cause of the disease, many people actually denied its very existence. Lack of support for the homosexual community spread out to the churches and families of the gay population. No one would discuss it, and many in the medical community refused to "put themselves in harm's way."

This was understandable. When AIDS first appeared no one knew how it was transmitted. It was also always terminal. Those two factors combined to terrify the medical community. The fear surrounding AIDS was paralyzing and immeasurable credit goes to the medical personnel who stood in the face of this danger to care for these patients.

I listened carefully to classes on protecting myself. I prayed to God to protect me if He wanted me to do this work. I let it go right there and joined the thousands of people dedicated to administering to those who were ill. As a result, I obtained a wealth of interpersonal gifts, so much more than I ever gave to anyone. Looking back, it was a transition in my life that I wouldn't change, no matter the price.

The first years of the crisis were difficult. The institutions one typically counts on were simply not responsive to those who were in need. Blood supplies were occasionally tainted with the AIDS virus and people became afraid to donate blood so supplies dwindled. Religious leaders who were supposed to be available were not just deaf, dumb, and blind but many arrogantly refused to even acknowledge there even was a crisis. From the pulpit, congregations were told that "no one in this church could ever have AIDS," and "AIDS is punishment from God to the gay community for their sins."

The sick were homeless in their religious communities and those who emotionally and physically cared for the sick were too angry to confront the faithful. Meanwhile the government was moving at its usual glacial pace. From where we stood the turmoil was palpable. Everywhere you turned you were fighting the conservative front, the medical world or the religious establishment. Many of these groups were beyond just being in denial — and no one yet knew the massive extent of this epidemic.

Years later Dennis came into my life.

There is an interesting part of New Jersey that sits high on a bluff overlooking Lower New York Harbor. In the evening you can easily see the lights of Manhattan. Because of its location it isn't a cheap place to live and has become the home of many well-to-do executives and business professionals. Homes hug the sides of the bluff as they precariously hang hundreds of feet above the bay.

Dennis was a hospice patient in our agency who owned an exquisite house with a phenomenal view. The house was built into the side of the bluff and from the expansive windows in the living room you could see the ocean, the harbor, and Manhattan. There was a dining room off the kitchen with two beautiful French doors that opened onto a wooden deck that was nearly as big as the house was. Giant trees shaded the deck, and the beautiful songs of hundreds of birds sweetly filled the air around the house. The view of Manhattan was unob-structed — and magnificent. In spite of the view, Dennis told me the favorite thing about living in this house was listening to the songs of the birds.

Dennis' parents called it his "bachelor pad."

Dennis was a twenty-eight year old professional. Successful in his career and friendships, he would later be acknowledged as an important, contributing part of his community. He had developed Karposi's Sarcoma, a particular type of cancer that manifests itself in AIDS patients. He lived alone but was well cared for by his partner and his friends.

Dennis would generally sleep all day and, like Aggie, be awake and in severe pain all night. It was difficult for the nursing team to manage his care because of this pattern, so in an effort to calm his anxiety I was asked to call him at night between 9:00 PM and 11:00 PM to reassure him and let him know we were available if he needed us. Before long, I was making late night visits for pain management. During this time we developed a wonderful, open, trusting relationship. This occurs frequently with members of the hospice team who enter their patient's lives and is one of those indescribable gifts people receive when working with the terminally ill.

Before long we were able to control Dennis' physical pain and teach his caregivers how to administer his medications and record them in the log book. The log book is crucial so we can track the amount of medication needed to control the pain. An accurate logbook is essential and allows us to adjust the long acting pain medication to a dosage that can control the pain for as long as possible.

Once his pain was under control and Dennis trusted that we would be there for him as he needed us, he was able to discuss the more important aspects of his pain. You see, Dennis had never told his parents he was gay. Time was running out and he did not want to die without telling them. He didn't want them believing he had simply 'died of cancer.' He wanted them to know the truth. At this point we brought in our medical social worker and our pastoral care minister. In many ways, they are the most valuable members of the hospice team. They were able to counsel and encourage Dennis to talk with his parents and they facilitated a family meeting so Dennis could ease his burden and be truthful with his mom and dad.

As difficult as it was, Dennis experienced tremendous relief once he was able to speak freely with his family. There was to be no more hiding of the facts — they now knew he had AIDS. Dennis' desire to have them aware and respectful of his partner was another major issue that was resolved easily without the anticipated pain that had begun to overwhelm Dennis.

Dennis reviewed his will with his parents and they assured him it would be honored according to his wishes.

With family issues out in the open and financial matters resolved, Dennis was now able to have some peaceful moments. He was able to talk about the terminal status of his illness but the spiritual aspect of his death still terrified him. He wasn't able to accept peace in his life and frequently felt tormented. *Perhaps this disease really was punishment from God*, he thought. Would he burn in Hell like many in the religious community were preaching? Who and what was God? Why had he been born? Endless questions attacked him with such an emotional fervor that we feared the virus had spread to his brain, as it often did with this disease.

Dennis' parents were now frequent visitors.

They lived in a nearby community known for its wealth and beauty. His parents were wonderful people who were comfortable with their wealth and felt no need to flaunt it. They had lived a fortunate life and were devastated that they had been left out of their son's life for so long. They were questioning every aspect of their lives and attitudes. Had they failed their son? Were they there for him when he needed them?

Dennis also confided in me that he felt he had brought shame to his family and his parents might not have been so accepting of his homosexuality had he not been terminally ill.

I was called to Dennis' home on a Tuesday night. His parents and his partner were all there with him. His pain was out of control and although I could have easily instructed everyone how to help Dennis, I felt the need to go there myself.

At 2:00 AM, in anyone's home, there is a special atmosphere that is difficult to describe. Whether in the presence of a king, celebrity or homeless person, the middle of the night is special. It is intimate and the masks we all wear during the day are removed by the peace the early morning brings. The patient, their care-givers, medical staff and family members all have their humanity exposed.

I got Dennis' pain under control fairly quickly and I wrote down dosage instructions and reviewed them with everyone.

I sat at the dining room table to write my report for Dennis' case managing nurse to read over in the morning. The lights of Manhattan, below me and far away, twinkled gently in the clear winter air. As I was finishing the report Dennis' parents came and sat with me. They were obviously in distress and it was evident they needed to talk to someone. They told me how they couldn't tell their pastor about their son's gay lifestyle or his disease. They were well aware of the stigma attached to his disease and they knew it wouldn't be received well. They were well-respected in their church community and even though they weren't afraid of what others would think of them, they still felt uncomfortable. They were angry that at such a horrific time in their lives, when they needed spiritual help, they didn't feel comfortable asking for it.

They felt comfortable to airing their concerns to me. As they spoke, I could see the determination return to their eyes. By the end of the conversation, they decided to confront their pastor and congregation with the truth. They felt someone had to speak out and open the door for future members of their church.

I told them I would ask the hospice pastoral minister to call them in the morning. "The minister can arrange a joint visit with you and her and your pastor," I told them. Satisfied they had support, they went home with a little more peace.

After they left, Dennis, his partner and I, sat in his living room discussing God and what was waiting for us after our deaths. We discussed the reason for our existence.

My belief system was now clearer and stronger than it had been at any other time in my life. I was well along in my journey of discovery and I was now comfortable discussing spirituality — my spirituality — with my patients and their families. My experiences as a hospice nurse had helped to crystallize my relationship with God.

Whether a patient personally believes in God or another deity, or is an atheist, makes no difference to me. I actually enjoy the differences of how we view this world and the possibility of what waits for us after death. With this in mind, the best I could do was confirm

Dennis' worth as a member of the human family. We discussed the possibility of this disease being for a larger purpose. Perhaps it would break down barriers and draw people closer to one another: parents to children, children to siblings, neighbors to neighbors.

The bottom line was that Dennis was not randomly put on this earth. If he was able to love and give of his talents to members of the community, surely this pleased God. We talked about life continuing after his body died and speculated whether he would continue to learn, grow, and serve.

Dennis's cancer had begun to metastasize rapidly, and tumors and ulcers were now visible on all parts of his body. In a strange way, this did not upset him. He felt he was being chosen to show the world this disease was real. There was no way to hide it. Dennis went for walks or to the store and generally continued to live his life as long as his body let him.

I have never met anyone who worked in hospice care who did not have unique experiences that gave them an increased understanding of living and dying. These experiences also force them to sincerely question if life continues after the body dies. There is little written on the subject, so everyone is basically left to draw their own conclusions. Hospice workers are at times able to discuss their spiritual experiences with coworkers, but for the most part they remain silent. We work in a world where people are either psychologically healthy or psychologically ill. No one wants to be cast into the latter group so most experiences remain unspoken and unwritten.

My contact with patients who were in the throes of a

spiritual crisis was now fairly frequent, so I was constantly bombarded with thoughts and questions of where we go when we leave this place.

A large reason I get to share my patients' spiritual thoughts and concerns is because of my late night shift. I mentioned the term "sun downing" earlier. This refers to a patient who can sleep comfortably during day but as soon as night falls they become wide awake. Symptoms become exacerbated and anxiety levels rise. Sleeping medications are not very effective and nighttime becomes a nightmare for these clients. There are multiple factors involved with sun downing.

During the day the world is awake and out and about, and the patient feels they can call for help and receive company. In general, the activity of the world is reassuring. At night they are left alone with their fears. Thoughts of death and punishment and tremendous fear plague these patients. Working the hours I worked, I came to see this more clearly. The hospice mantra of "relieving physical symptoms so the important work can be done" had a clear meaning to me.

I told Dennis about other patients in his situation. I also reassured him that what he was going through was not unique and more importantly, it was not a sign of mental illness, which he feared he was succumbing to.

I asked him to give me a sign if at the time of his death the other side was all he believed it to be. If it was a place of love and life and acceptance, I told him a sign would be a great gift to those of us he had left behind. I asked him to give the sign so that whoever was in atten-dance would clearly know it came from the spirit world. Dennis agreed to do this if he had the power to accomplish it. We agreed that a lack of a sign wouldn't indicate he was not well.

I left Dennis' home at peace with the world. I felt blessed, and so did my patient and his loved ones.

It would be several days before I saw Dennis again, although I continued to call at the start of my shift to make sure things were all right. The following Monday I returned to my home just before midnight after visiting another patient. I got into bed looking forward to a good night's rest, but at 3:00 AM I woke up and was unable to get back to sleep. I decided to take a shower and get dressed. My intuition was now in charge.

At three-thirty the phone rang. Dennis' mother said his breathing was changing and he was asking for a visit. I told her Dennis was probably starting the dying process and he needed a calm environment.

We had left the family with various brochures and written materials telling them what to expect. They were aware of the normal signs of the dying process but like many others in the same position, when the time actually arrived, they needed reassurance.

I got to Dennis' home within the hour but he had died before I got there. After completing the pronouncement procedure, I asked permission to wash Dennis and dress him to leave his home for the last time. Dennis' family and partner stayed with him for a while before they let me prepare him.

Dawn was about to break and while I was busy with Dennis his family decided to go out to the balcony and watch the sun rise. A few minutes later, as the sun climbed up over the ocean, I was called out to the living room with great urgency by his father.

I got to the French doors and was shocked by what I saw — my breath was taken away. The three-sided rail on the balcony was covered with red cardinals! Sitting side by side they were looking into Dennis' home. The amount of them amazed us — there wasn't room for one more cardinal! The deck was at least twenty feet long and ten feet wide — that meant that there were forty feet of feather-to-feather cardinals, with each one looking at the exact same spot in Dennis' living room. No one could figure out exactly what these hundreds of birds were looking at, but whatever it was they were all intent on it!

His parents told me Dennis had discussed with them the request I had made for a sign. Although they did not believe it was possible, they were hopeful a confirmation their son was alive and accepted after death would come to them. We stared at the birds and cried and laughed. We were in awe of Dennis' power and generosity after his death.

For a moment in time, all of us were treated to a glimpse of the continuation of love and life. Goodbye and thank you Dennis. Your sign gave us joy and peace.

Chapter 10. Barney.

When I think about Pasha, I think about the gorgeous, energetic, raven-haired child I was introduced to the first time I visited her family. She was by all appearances a healthy, rambunctious four year old.

I had moved and was working in a new agency. This agency had never taken pediatric patients before but was now beginning to accept them for hospice care. Because of my experience with children I was chosen to case manage Pasha. I was now able to comfortably deal with things I had always been afraid of.

In the densely populated suburbs of central New Jersey, in the midst of large concentrations of mixed housing units and ringed by major highways, is a college town that is a true melting pot. In late October, on a winsome autumn afternoon, I traveled there to meet Pasha for the first time.

In spite of my experience, I am always still afraid I won't be capable of managing a child's symptoms. In this case, those fears were unnecessary because I had wonderful help from Pasha's Pediatric Oncologist who was more than willing to teach and guide me.

I also still fear I won't be able to keep my own emotions in check. I prayed all the way to the child's home that I would not cry in front of her family. Children tug at my heart, and even when I know their illness is incurable, it never changes the fact that I pray for a miracle for every new patient.

My beliefs were still developing. I didn't fully understand the age of a spiritual being and I did not understand that I was supposed to learn lessons from this child. I didn't know that sometimes a life was to be lived for a day, or a year, or five years, and that it all had a purpose. I did not understand that we, the survivors, were meant to learn lessons from every soul we encounter.

I still had a difficult time dealing with the death of children. I was driven only by my belief that children deserve to have their symptoms relieved. I functioned on faith and brut determination. As I was evolving and growing I was becoming able to put myself aside, step out of the way, and allow the child and her family to lead me in the pursuit of treatment and support.

I entered the home and introduced myself. Pasha's mother and father were from India. Pasha's mother was educated and her father was a student at the local university.

As we sat at the kitchen table in their small and tidy apartment, I explained the role hospice would play in their child's life. "Your doctor suggested we meet so I can explain hospice care and you can then decide if you wish to have this service. Hospice care is basically in-home care. The focus is on managing Pasha's pain, breathing difficulties and any anxiety she might experience. We'll be here to help with anything that might come up as we work to keep Pasha as comfortable as possible. The focus is not to cure your child's illness. The nursing staff will visit a few times a week, or more if you need them. A nurse will be available twenty-four hours a day to answer questions and make a visit if necessary."

"What if our doctor wants to send her for experimental treatment?" Pasha's father asked. Pasha's mother and father were very quiet and reserved, but their calm demeanor belied their turmoil and incredible sadness.

"We'll simply discharge Pasha from hospice. You determine the plan of care for your daughter and we follow your lead. Hospice care can be terminated anytime you want." It was my job to explain the facts to Pasha's parents and not to persuade them to follow one treatment path over another.

Pasha had been diagnosed with a glioblastoma — a brain tumor. She had already undergone two surgeries to relieve the pressure on her brain by removing as much of the tumor as possible, but the tumor could not be completely removed. After a long period of stability, the tumor was again growing and it was only a matter of time before Pasha would succumb.

"We are afraid we will not know how to care for Pasha. We are not doctors and do not know what to expect."

"We understand that. One of the functions of hospice is to teach you how to care for her. We'll teach you in your home and be available over the phone. We can change the treatment if new symptoms arise. Whether it's two in the morning or two in the afternoon, we'll be available for you." I explained the other support services available: home health aides, social workers for emotional support, pastoral care and other support volunteers. At this time they only wanted the nurse. That wasn't a problem since parents are permitted to add or subtract services as they please.

"Our biggest fear is that our child will suffer. We do not want her in a hospital suffering. We want her comfortable and at home." It was a request I had sadly heard many times before but each time I heard it, it stabbed me as if it was the first time.

"That's our goal too and we'll do whatever we can to make sure that happens."

Although Pasha was unable to play like a healthy four year old, she was still fairly active. She had several cousins her own age who visited her on a regular basis. Even though she always had plenty of playmates and company, she very rarely left the house.

She loved her Teletubby and Barney videos and the toys she had from those programs.

The family received an average of three visits a week and gradually they accepted the assistance of the home health aide, social worker and even the pastoral care. Slowly they were accepting help and understanding that our goal was to help them—not to dictate how that help was delivered. Trusting people outside of their culture and network of friends and family was difficult, but they eventually embraced our help.

They were immigrants and were very private. They were used to being with other members of the local Indian community. Since they had only been in this country for a short time they had not yet assimilated into the mainstream.

Pasha's father never even told his professors or department head that his daughter was terminally ill. He simply reached out to his family because they were not used to asking for help from outsiders. We had made a major step forward in helping the family just by being permitted to enter their lives.

Pasha's condition progressed rapidly. We received many phone calls asking for clarification about certain things or asking about increased pain symptoms or fatigue. With help from the hospice team and Pasha's doctor we were able to keep Pasha fairly comfortable throughout all of the changes. As Pasha's condition got worse we were in daily contact with her parents.

Her mother told me one day she was very concerned

about Pasha after her death. "Could you tell me about cremation in this country?"

I wasn't totally sure I knew what information she was looking for. "How is cremation in your country?" I asked her.

"In my country bodies are cremated in the open according to our religious beliefs."

"There is no open cremation in this country." I explained the cremation process to her. "Do you want Pasha to be cremated?" I asked.

"No, I'm not comfortable with cremating Pasha at all. Even though it is our custom, I hate the thought of it. What else can I do?"

I explained the burial procedure in this country as well as embalming.

"My husband would not put up with burial."

"Have you discussed it with him?"

"No. I could not," she said. I could see the distress in her eyes.

"Would you mind if I opened the discussion with him?"

"No, it would be all right." She seemed relieved and the conversation ended there.

Later in the week, when her husband and his male relatives were gathered in the living room, I asked him about burying Pasha.

"We have decided that Pasha will be cremated according to the custom in this country," he said flatly as if he wasn't interested in discussing the subject any further.

"Have you discussed this with your wife? She's disturbed about the thought of Pasha being cremated," I said.

This came as a shock to him. In India this would not even have been a consideration. Even though there is a great deal of respect between the sexes and family always comes first, the men in the family make the decisions about such things. To change tradition in response to Pasha's mother's concerns about her cremation was simply unheard of.

"I think you should speak with your wife about this. It's important that you are both comfortable about your decisions after Pasha dies. The decisions you make now will affect you both for the rest of your lives."

The next day Pasha's mother and father thanked me and told me they wanted to look into an "American burial" for their daughter. I gave Pasha's father directions to a company where they could look at and purchase a casket. Pasha's father and his male relatives visited the company who supplied them a casket at cost. They had decided to listen to Pasha's mother and honor her concerns—this was a big deal!

Eventually the social worker and pastoral care minister met with the couple and helped them formulate a burial that was acceptable to them both.

Pasha's parents' religion teaches that we are all reincarnated after death, but neither had been raised devoutly and they did not have a strong religious base to lean on. They considered themselves religiously affiliated based on their culture and heritage rather than through knowledge they had sought out and obtained as adults. Like so many of us, they believed what they believed because of the way they were raised. It was easy for me to talk to them about this as they were really no different than I was.

We discussed the possibility that death does not actually occur because the spirit continues to live on. Pasha's parents believed in reincarnation and believed a person goes "back home" for encouragement and guidance. They believed we all receive help from the other side.

During one of these conversations I brought up the signs I had received from other patients. "These signs don't prove anything except that the sign was asked for and given," I said.

"Wouldn't that be something if Pasha could do that?" Pasha's mother said. She was truly excited at the prospect.

The conversation ended with all of us thinking "wouldn't it be nice?" and "how interesting it would be if Pasha could send us a sign," but it wasn't something her parents actually believed could happen. Besides, Pasha was only four, how could she understand what we were asking her to do?

Even though I had seen it with the babies, I still did not fully realize the truth about the age of the soul. I wasn't yet convinced that we couldn't put the age of a spirit into particular lengths of time like we do with our own birthdays here on earth.

As the weeks progressed Pasha started showing signs her tumor was actively growing again. One night I received a frantic call from her mother. Pasha was having a seizure. Her mother was familiar with the symptoms because Pasha had had seizures before and after her previous surgeries. We had been aware of the probability of their occurrence and had left suppositories to calm the symptoms down. I instructed her mother how to use the medication and then got in my car for the forty-minute drive to their home.

When I got there, Pasha was calm and walking around with her little cousin. She even felt well enough to have a little tug-of-war over her Barney doll. I reviewed the medications and left after telling her parents that the seizures might appear more frequently as the tumor progressed. "Don't hesitate to call us, no matter what time it is," I said as I put my coat on and walked toward the door.

Not quite a week later we received a call that Pasha had had three seizures in twenty-four hours. I called her doctor and he determined that Pasha should receive the seizure medication on a regularly scheduled basis. This wasn't done to stop the seizures — it was too late for that, but at least we could lessen their severity.

I explained this to her mother. She understood and adhered to the schedule despite the fact that Pasha was becoming more fatigued and lethargic. "I hate to see my little girl so tired; she hardly wants to play anymore. I'm afraid of what is to come," she said.

"She'll become more fatigued as the disease progresses but I assure you that we'll keep the pain and seizures under control. If, at any time, you want to bring Pasha back to the hospital you have the right to do so."

"No, I just want her to stay a little longer. I'm not ready to let her go."

That afternoon I called the social worker and requested she make a visit to help the family finalize the burial plans. Plans were made for a home viewing to be followed by a service at the funeral home and then the burial at a cemetery about fifteen miles away. Since the family had no familiarity with this process they needed our guidance every step of the way.

Pasha died peacefully and I was privileged to be with her at the time of her death. Pasha died in her mother's arms while her father held her mother. After I pronounced the death, Pasha's mother and her female relatives bathed and dressed her while the men of the family brought the tiny white casket into the living room. Pasha was then placed in the casket along with her beloved and well-used Barney doll. I left their home confident that everything was going to be taken care of properly.

We arrived at the funeral home the following morning and found an abundance of beautiful pink roses surrounding Pasha's casket. The hospice minister said prayers for Pasha and her family. Everyone said their goodbyes to Pasha as her parents added a rose to the casket and then kissed their sweet daughter and her Barney goodbye.

It was a bitterly cold February day with a stiff wind that added to everyone's misery. Pasha's coffin was placed in the hearse and everyone was instructed to put their lights on and stay close together for the journey to the cemetery.

I was filled with awe. Here we were, hospice staff of many different backgrounds and beliefs being allowed by this family to guide them in the care and burial of their precious daughter.

Sometimes blessings are so strong all you can do is be still and allow them to enter you.

A strong wind blew across the open expanse of the cemetery as everyone gathered for the graveside service. The tiny little casket rested above the open grave on the straps used to lower it into the ground after the service. The casket swayed in the strong wind and I was beginning to panic. I was afraid the wind would knock the casket over. Several of the men grabbed hold of the casket and kept it from falling over.

Usually those in attendance say a final prayer, place a flower on the casket and then leave the grave before it is lowered into the ground. We explained the meaning of all of this to the family and realized the size of the blessing we had received. This entire family had handed over their precious Pasha to us for safe-keeping—what a statement of trust!

Because of the wind and their desire to be a complete part of Pasha's farewell, the men decided to lower the casket into the ground immediately following the service. This was a wonderful show of love and respect for Pasha's mother, especially since they had all decided on cremation before Pasha's mother voiced her concerns.

After the casket was safely lowered into the grave, the women were all escorted back to their cars while the men remained graveside and they replaced all of the dirt back into the grave. I stayed with the funeral director and his assistant while Pasha's casket was covered.

I returned to my office after the ceremony and shortly after arriving I received a call from Pasha's mother. One of Pasha's little cousins — a child of three — came into the house carrying Pasha's Barney!

"She must have had her own," I said.

"No!" Pasha's mother replied. "The foot was threadbare and the arm was loose. It was Pasha's doll. And Pasha's cousin came from South America with her parents just last night. They never purchased a Barney toy for her."

I asked Pasha's mother if she had called the funeral director to see if the casket had somehow been opened after it left the funeral home. She said she had checked with the funeral director and the casket had not been opened after it was placed in the hearse. After it was removed from the hearse I was with the casket until after it had been placed in the ground and covered over with dirt. I knew for certain that no one had opened the casket!

Pasha, thank you for allowing me into your life and thank you for your sign. We will never forget that indeed death is only for a moment and your spirit is alive and caring for us all.

Chapter 11. Swings.

The care of a terminally ill patient is always sad and difficult. Some people look at members of the hospice staff and think we have a special gift. They wonder how we do our work, how we are not depressed or sad all of the time. I will tell you that I am not any more special than the average person. Everyone I have ever met who works in this field isn't any more special than anyone else. The only thing special about us is that we dare to enter the world of the dying. This does not mean we do not hurt, become anxious, or question why we do the work we do. No, it just means we have dared to do something we feel driven to do.

An interesting fact about this field is that staff members rarely get fired. They either have a passion to learn and do the work or they can't take it and leave.

For whatever reason we have chosen this profession, there are always times that it hurts so bad we wonder why we do it.

Our office received a call from the Pediatric Oncologist in a nearby city about a four year old child who was no longer responding to treatment. The doctor requested we meet with the parents and explain the benefits of the hospice program so they could determine if it was the course of treatment they wanted for their son.

There was no one else on our staff who had experience case managing a terminally ill child. Although I was now becoming accustomed to this in our small agency, I wanted to pass this time. I recently had case managed two children and I needed an emotional rest. It is interesting to me that when an experience is important to our growth, no matter what we want or how well we rationalize our need to avoid it, we are confronted with the situation. I was assigned to case manage Alex.

Driving to Alex's home, I really tried to relax. Deep breathing usually works for me and all the way there I practiced it.

Alex's parents were young and devoted to their family and their children. As parents, they were simply too young to be put through this sadness that had entered their lives.

Alex was small for his age. His infrequent smile and weak body were a testament to the illness ravaging his little body.

His brother was eight years old and for the past two years—a quarter of his life—he had been living with a little brother who was becoming sicker and weaker by the day.

Where there had been hope, now there was only waiting. Where the parents' attention had been focused on one more doctor, one more medical center to find the cure, now there was only waiting.

As the parents gave me Alex's medical history a story of frustration and sadness unfolded. Alex had developed seizures at age two. Diagnosed with epilepsy, his mom and dad were confident his condition could be controlled. When the seizures continued despite medication, they felt like they had failed their son. Had they chosen the wrong doctor? Not paid enough attention to the instructions for giving the medication? After all, epilepsy was a relatively common disorder and many children live a fairly stable life with this disease. Why couldn't they control Alex's seizures despite the medical care he received?

They told me how his behavior gradually changed, and how he had become hyperactive. He was on the go all day and needed to be held frequently to calm him down. Because he was disruptive and a danger to the other children, his day care program could no longer accept his behavior. Alex had been in day care because his mother and father both needed to work to make ends meet, but his mother eventually left her job to stay at home until Alex's seizures could be controlled.

His mother encouraged him to color in books and create pictures with his water color set. Alex loved to create pictures of bluebirds and told his family the birds were his friends. There were pictures of bluebirds taped all over the walls of Alex's bedroom.

"Never once did we suspect this would turn into a terminal disease," she said as she wiped a tear from her eye.

Eventually Alex's behavior became even stranger. While driving down a street Alex would spot a swing and demand to get out and play. It didn't matter that the swing was in someone's backyard. He became uncontrollable if his demands were not met. His parents became experts on every school yard and park swing in the area in order to avoid Alex's fits. He was also the same way with sprinklers but nothing else affected him in the same manner.

Eventually, Alex's doctor made a referral to a Pediatric Neurological Hospital in New York City. After extensive testing they diagnosed a rare cancer and told them that a deep brain tumor was interfering with the neurological function of the brain. The anti-seizure medications were appropriate but would not cure him. Sadly, there was no cure, as the location of the tumor rendered it inoperable.

Assured that they had exhausted all medical options,

Alex's parents now wanted information on hospice protocols. I explained to the parents that the goal of hospice care was symptom control and the maintenance of the highest quality of life possible. If they wanted to hospitalize Alex, we would discharge him from the program and readmit him upon discharge from the hospital. "We don't have hard and fast rules for children. You head up the plan of care and we follow it."

Alex's parents were clear — they wanted Alex to remain at home and they wanted no further hospitalization, no feeding tubes and no artificial life support.

They knew Alex was going to die and they were only concerned with his comfort. I assured them that we wouldn't use injections and we wouldn't cause any pain in the effort to soothe his symptoms. I explained the role of the nurse, social worker, minister and volunteer and they were eager to utilize all of the services available to them.

I frequently needed to speak with the doctor at the New York hospital to titrate the doses of medications for Alex's headaches, seizures and respiratory problems, and I eventually became comfortable with his care and confident in my ability. Over a four month period, Alex's condition didn't significantly change. His weakness was increasing and he now needed to be diapered and fed, but he was fairly stable. Although I had grown more comfortable caring for Alex I still dreaded what was to come. Would I be capable of providing sufficient care?

Although it may seem like one nurse cares for a patient, it takes many people for that one person to effectively do their job. Thanks to my wonderful hospice staff, anyone I needed for consultation or emotional support was available to me. The physician who was the director of our hospice was gracious and was available whenever I needed him. Although Alex was seen by two other nurses during his time with us, I was the on-call nurse and was responsible to handle any emergencies.

I had several conversations with his parents regarding their plan for Alex's burial. They had decided not to have a traditional burial. They wanted Alex to be cremated with no church service. Alex's mother was Jewish and his father's family was fundamentalist Christian and there was a great deal of contention regarding Alex's care. Both sets of grandparents fervently imposed their religious beliefs on Alex's family. Because of this, Alex's parents didn't receive the support they so critically needed during the most difficult time in their lives.

Alex's maternal grandmother insisted on being there twenty-four hours a day, seven days a week, and although she meant to be helpful she was smothering Alex and his family. Alex's paternal grandparents insisted that Alex was going to die because his parents lacked faith. The burden the grandparents laid on Alex's parents was overwhelming.

Visits by either set of grandparents weren't helpful in the least. Instead of giving Alex's parents a chance to rest, they became stressful events that were dreaded instead of looked forward to. Arguments occurred frequently and although family was still welcome, visits were seriously curtailed. I could feel the tension as they discussed the situation.

With the help of the hospice social worker and minister, Alex's parents planned a memorial service for him. With this out of the way, Alex's parents and big brother were a little more relaxed. They told their families that they had to respect the decision that had been made, and grudgingly it was accepted.

Eventually, Alex's disease progressed to the point that we knew he would not be able to sustain life for much longer. He was eating the equivalent of a jar of baby food a day and taking only sips of fluids. He was too weak to hold his head up. His doctor confirmed his condition was not reversible and the symptoms would continue until Alex's death.

I continued educating his parents about medications and emergency procedures like choking. In spite of the difficulties they now had caring for Alex, his parents continually told me that they did not want hospitalization or life support. Parents lead the way. They will never be criticized for their decisions and our role is simply to support those decisions.

Probably because of the length of Alex's care in hospice, I came to know his mother very well. We would sit and talk not only about Alex and his care but other topics as well. Alex's mother confided in me as she would a trusted friend. I was overwhelmed by her faith in me. Eventually the topic of the sign arose during a discussion related to their lack of religious involvement and the dissension within their family. I resigned myself to the truth: *there would be no sign in this case*. Alex was too young to understand and too ill to comprehend even basic information.

I still was not completely confident with what I had learned from Pasha and the babies about the age of one's spirit and I still did not fully realize that our spirit hears and understands all. Alex was indeed concerned with his family's grief but that knowledge hadn't yet entered into my life.

As Alex weakened I was called to the home almost daily. Now my prayer was that I be available at the time of his death. My prayers were answered when I received the call from Alex's mother to come immediately as his breathing was slowing. I arrived just in time to witness Alex's death.

"Is it happening now?" his mother asked me.

"Yes. Call your husband and have your neighbor bring Danny home from school."

They wanted Alex's brother home when Alex died. They felt that excluding him might cause him unnecessary fear and anxiety. Danny might wonder how his brother died, what death looks like, and if Alex was in pain when he died.

If a child can have a good death, Alex certainly did. With no discomfort or severe symptoms, he died softly in his mother's arms.

For the next hour she continued to hold Alex but eventually she decided the family should go for a ride while the funeral director came for him. They didn't want Danny's last memory of his little brother to be one as sad as watching him be taken away in a hearse. Alex's mother handed Alex to me before she left because she wanted Alex to spend as much time as possible being held and cared for. They went to visit friends who lived nearby and left the phone number in case I needed it. "I know you'll take good care of him for me," she said as they left.

It had been raining heavily all day. *How appropriate it is to be raining on the day this child was dying!* I thought as I watched his family leave. I was left alone with Alex. *What an incredible gift for these parents to trust me with their precious son.* Alex's mother put him in my arms and I held and rocked him while I waited for the funeral director. My heart was heavy and again I struggled with a God who could not or would not intervene to heal this child. What possible good would there be in Alex's death? I respected God but I must confess I did not understand and I did not feel guilty about my lack of understanding.

All of the funeral arrangements had already been

made and all the consents had been signed. Thirty minutes passed while I sat alone with Alex—a long hard thirty minutes. How could I put him down, for any reason, if his parents had faith I would hold him? The young man from the funeral home arrived and was visibly shaken by the sight of such a young child. I gave him the phone number where his parents were. He called them and then he took Alex from my arms.

It was interesting to me that the funeral director did not bring in a stretcher for Alex but carried him out in his arms. I stood thinking how really good people are and watched this man who was now receiving a blessing in his kind act.

Once Alex was gone I called his parents. They said they would be right home and I waited for them as I didn't want to leave their home unattended. Five minutes after calling them the rain stopped. *Was our grief to be eased?* I thought sarcastically. My continued lack of understanding and anger was bubbling up from deep inside.

They came in the door a few minutes later. It was a terribly sad moment and his brother was visibly shaken. A very short while later Danny called for his parents. He was in the bedroom crying as he looked out the window to the back yard. The sun was shining and there was no wind and yet the swing was swinging high, back and forth as if it was being maniacally pushed by an invisible hand! It was mid-February—too early for robins in New Jersey—yet one was perched on the windowsill, peering in at us!

Alex's parents were amazed and cried and smiled as they realized that Alex had spoken to them to let them know he was all right and still a part of their family.

I had thought that a child in Alex's condition would

be unable to send us a sign, but my lack of understanding does not change the nature and ability of a spirit. Sometimes the most telling communication comes in the form of an unexpected sign.

Thank you Alex and thank you to the other side. Your concern for those left behind was a subject at the two hospice memorials that Alex's parents and big brother participated in. You have given comfort to many people who were filled with sadness beyond their ability to comprehend. We will never forget you and your sign. We who cared about you in hospice were left with the knowledge that we know close to nothing about life and death and that has helped us in our own journeys.

Chapter Twelve. Return.

It had been a draining week and I was looking forward to two sorely needed days off. I was hoping this particular Friday night would be a quiet one. It almost happened.

It had been raining really hard all day and into the evening. I was just beginning to think I'd be able to stay put for the night when I got a call to visit a patient who lived in a rural area in another part of the state.

"Hello, dear, could you come out to see me tonight?" the soft, elderly voice asked me.

I had never met this patient or worked on her case, so I had to look through her records and the nurse's log before I could leave.

Thirty-five miles doesn't seem far but most of the journey is on side roads. This is funny and tells you something about myself. If I go to an urban area in the middle of the night, even in a "bad" neighborhood, I have no fear. Send me to a rural, sparsely populated area after dark and it makes me very anxious. One time my anxiety was so bad I called and woke up my supervisor and asked her to help me. She stayed on the phone with me and talked me through my journey until I arrived at my destination.

The way to Margaret's home was through unlit farm areas with poorly marked streets. In the dark it's easy to become lost — especially in the rain.

Before I left I checked the daily log and saw that Margaret had clinically died earlier in the day, but had been revived. Margaret was in her eighties and lived with her elderly sister, who was alone with her and was certain she had died. Her sister called hospice and asked us to come out and do a pronouncement. The day shift nurse got to the house a short while later and began the pronouncement procedure. During the pronouncement Margaret revived and her vital signs stabilized. The nurse gave her something for her anxiety as Margaret was somewhat agitated, and then left the home.

I didn't know what to expect when I got there and I spent the trip switching between trying to keep from getting lost and trying to psyche myself up so I could help this patient—no matter what she needed. Needless to say, it was a long and anxiety-laden trip out to the beautiful countryside of central New Jersey.

I was so fatigued I was afraid I wouldn't be of any help to anyone as I squinted between the raindrops and windshield wipers, looking for Margaret's home. I parked in front of her house after finding it on my second trip down her street.

Her two-story home was very old and quite small. It was situated in the middle of a tiny village that had been settled in the 18th century. Surrounded by miles and miles of farms, about twelve old homes were clustered close together. There was still an operating post office on the first floor of one home and one old mill in town had been converted into a restaurant. This little village is a quiet throwback to a way of life that has been disappearing rapidly from the rural landscape throughout the country.

Margaret greeted me at the door of her enclosed porch. She was very frail but was a woman of dignity. She was dressed neatly and her home was in order.

"Are you in any pain or discomfort?" I asked after I greeted her and entered the porch. It was early spring and still quite chilly but Margaret's enclosed porch was heated and comfortable. We stayed there and spoke without going into the house.

"No," Margaret replied, "my medication is working very well but thank you for asking. I called you here because I needed to talk about my experience today."

Margaret's sister came and introduced herself and told me that Margaret had been doing well since the afternoon. "I put water on for tea for you two. I'm going to go up to bed. Goodnight now," she said as she left the porch.

"Perhaps you'd like to wait until the morning?" I asked Margaret after her sister left. "I could have your regular nurse come out first thing in the morning." Margaret had never even called to ask a question at night, let alone request a visit. I was concerned for her.

"No dear," she said. "I need to speak with you right away. You see, I feel pressure to speak to you right away."

Margaret didn't know me, but it still seemed like when she said 'I need to speak to *you* right away,' she meant *me* specifically. "Who?" I asked. "Who's pressuring you?"

"The other side," she responded. "You know my dear, I grew up in this town. I've attended the church down the street all my life. We believe in the Bible. If it's not in the Bible, it's not the truth. It's been very simple for me all my life. I know I am going to die soon and I am not afraid of death. This cancer has caused me a lot of distress. I was actually praying for my death so I could leave my sick body behind. I'm done with it, it served its purpose well but now it is just too sick and painful. I don't want to be here anymore. I left here today but had to come back. I had to come back to speak with you."

The nurse in me came out as I searched for reassurance that the hospice team and doctor had done all they could to keep her comfortable.

"I'm very pleased with all the care I received. They took very good care of me and whenever I called, they came. They did not want me in pain and when I complained they took care of the pain. But you know dear, it is not easy, after all these years, having strangers in your home. I never called them unless the pain was so bad it made me cry."

"Oh, I wish you hadn't felt that way. The nurses could have saved you from that misery."

"It's okay, dear, I like my privacy. My, my, between the lady who washed me and did my hair, the nurse, the counselor and the minister, I could have had someone here all the time. I'm not used to that kind of fussing. Everyone was so dear. They would talk to me. They wanted to know if I was afraid of death. They prayed with me. They were just so dear. But I never really told them anything, I just agreed with them to make them think I was all right."

"Why did you do that?" I asked.

"They have enough work to do without worrying about me. I didn't want to trouble them. And to tell you the truth, I never thought much about death or God. I just learned what I was told and left it at that.

She went on to tell me about her experience that day.

"I knew I had died. I saw everything. I saw my sister sitting next to my bed and the nurse was there too. She was checking me. I was up high out of my body but I was still me. I left my room and found myself in a wonderful place. I was young and healthy, happy and energetic. I can't describe to you how beautiful the place I was in was.

"I saw other people and met with a, I guess you could say, a 'spiritual being' who loved me. This spirit, or being, told me that it wasn't my time to come there yet. I was terribly disappointed and asked why and I was told I still had work to do. I had to let people know that death isn't the end and that we keep living after our death on earth. I had to tell people what a wonderful place was waiting for us." She smiled a beautiful and peaceful smile, as if she was enjoying the memory of her wonderful visit.

"Then I felt myself coming back down into my body. I need you to tell them that I really did die. When I realized I was fully back in my body I became very upset. I hated it! I wanted to go back. I was angry. I thought there had been a mistake. The nurse gave me medication and I went to sleep."

"Margaret, were you afraid?" I asked her.

"No dear, just the opposite, I was fine and free, healthy and young."

"Why did you need to tell me this story tonight?" I asked.

"I just needed to call and have you come here."

"But Margaret, we've never met before. Why did you feel the need to tell me?"

"Yes dear. You see, you need to know what death is like. You need to know that God is real just like you and me. He is as real as we are. God gives us angels and guides to watch over us and help us throughout our lives. They help us and encourage us when we need it. They even educate us. I found out we are here on earth to accomplish tasks and learn from them so we can become more like God and teach others about God through our actions. I learned we never die. We are spirit beings and while we're here on earth we take on a human body, but we are spirit beings. We never die. Our spirits are the same as we are."

"Who told you this?" I asked.

"No one told me, I just learned it while I was there."

"What happens to us?"

"Oh, we leave our bodies on the earth. Why, we have no more care for them then we would for old, ripped clothing. Our new bodies are us but beautiful and younger."

"We get a new body after we die?" I asked. I was fascinated by how real her experience was to her.

"Yes, but they are our spirit body, our real body. It's not heavy like our earth body and doesn't need the care our earth body needs. After I left here I was no longer old. I was younger and I could stand up straight! I was confident and unafraid."

She told me that we take our emotions and thinking with us to the other side.

"Margaret, what happens if we die unhappy or can't accept that we have died? What if we don't want to die?" I thought this was a silly question, but maybe she knew the answer to something I had often wondered about.

"If we die and are not in harmony with our spirit we obtain help from those on the other side. We are cared for and receive guidance until we are well."

What does one say to this? I was shocked. Her answers came easily, as if she had been filled with this knowledge all of her life.

Margaret was becoming visibly tired but still wanted to talk.

"Margaret, why did you come back?" I asked.

"I came back to finish my work and to tell you the other side is real. You see I didn't really believe this all my life, but now I know."

"Who is this information for?" I asked.

"Why dear, it's for you. That's why I called you. It's for you and those you wish to share it with." Margaret was exhausted. "Please young lady, get us some tea and come sit by me."

I did just that. We shared a cup of tea while I relished her company and felt a high energy in the room. It's difficult to explain except to say I know it had become a sacred place—a place of peace and honor. I thought it was a place I didn't deserve to be in, but her words made me change my mind. *I must deserve to be here or I would not have been the one this woman called for.*

"Thank you Margaret, for sharing this information with me. I'm honored to be with you tonight."

"Thank you for listening to me and caring about what I had to tell you. I'm tired. I want to lie down on the couch now."

I placed an afghan over her and put her favorite music on her record player. I turned down the volume and lowered the lights. I sat on the floor next to her and held her hand. *Such a fragile hand, almost like that of a young child.*

"Goodnight dear," she said, "and lock the door behind you when you leave."

She never took another breath.

Thank you Margaret. You sealed my faith and took away my fear. I will honor your experience and share it with others.

Epilogue. Spirit.

What is spirit? What is the soul?

This was always a difficult concept for me to understand. Raised with a religious background I was taught the soul is formless. It returns to either heaven or hell after death.

My journey has helped me enlarge my personal understanding of the soul. It is who we are. It is me and it is you. It is exactly us. It will maintain my attitude, my memories, my viewpoints, my laughter, my self.

To understand your spirit, think about what takes away your self. When you have your hair cut and some of your hair rests on the floor, have you lost part of yourself? When you trim your fingernails have you lost part of yourself? When you have an appendectomy, do you remain your self? If you lose your arm does your self remain?

Inch by inch, my body can be modified and parts removed and my self remains. So what is my *self*? It is my spirit. It is not a wisp of a cloud that floats to an unknown place, above the known universe where it melds with all the other wisps of clouds. No, I believe my self — your self — never stops existing.

How do I know this is correct? I am not a scholar or spiritualist and I have no psychic abilities. I am a nurse who earns her living caring for patients with serious symptoms that affect the quality of their everyday lives — patients who have life-threatening illnesses or who are dying.

Growing up, and later as an adult, I was taught repeatedly that we as humans are not worthy to meet God because we are dirty flesh. We are born, live in inferiority, and die to be sentenced to either Heaven or Hell. Only the righteous get into Heaven and no man is righteous, so where does that leave us?

Working with my patients and their loved ones, I have learned from them by what I witnessed and by what I dared ask them to show me. This book is a journal of my experiences with many different types of patients. Different ages, ethnic backgrounds, different religious beliefs. I have included only a few of the most profound experiences I have had. Over the years I have seen many, many, wonderful and mysterious things that would take volumes to recount. But through it all there is one constant: the most powerful thing I have learned is that once you have the courage to ask, your questions usually result in answers.

I have been changed by the experiences I have shared with you. For me, there is no longer any fear of death. I have stopped worrying about the future and I have learned to embrace every moment as it comes. I have learned to embrace *now*. Wondrous moments are available to all of us if we learn to trust what we are experiencing. I have learned not to seek validation but to hold my patient's and their family's experiences as their truth.

This book is not meant to "prove" the existence of life after death, but to record the experiences of some of my patients. I suppose "proof" happens when this type of experience is the norm. I suspect the truth is these experiences are the norm but witnesses to them remain silent.

I thank you for your time and for allowing me to share these experiences with you. I am sure that most of us have had spiritual experiences related to the passing of a loved one. I would welcome you to share those experiences with me. Together we can open the door to greater understanding.

You may contact me at shiprock88@aol.com via email or regular mail through my publisher at the following address:

Patricia Thoms
c/o Cloonfad Press
PO Box 106
Cassville, NJ, 08527